The wave of heat hit me in the
across the room, slamming me he
I hit the floor and lay there for
oughly confused at what had just happened. My hand stung sharply, and I looked down to find it had reddened like bad sunburn. I looked up at Alleam and my breath caught in my throat.

He was standing in the middle of the room as before, one hand raised. He was surrounded by a near-dazzling glow of blue-white energy, as if his very aura had been set alight. His eyes were shining bright blue and his lips were twisted in a grimace that was aimed directly at me. After a moment, the glow in his eyes faded and the halo of light disappeared. He lowered his hand slowly and surveyed me with a look that bordered on impatience.

I pushed myself to my feet, suddenly feeling scared and very vulnerable. The gun was still lying on my desk but by this point I hardly dared to move. I just stood, gaping open-mouthed at Alleam with a million questions rushing through my head. Eventually I found my voice and shakily asked, "What the hell are you?"

Alleam stared at me for a long moment, ignoring the expletive. "I'm an angel," he said simply. "And you're going to help me stop the Apocalypse."

Conquest

Book 1 of the Angels of Chicago series

C.J. Somersby

Dagda
Publishing

Copyright © C.J. Somersby 2015
Cover Design Copyright © Matt Davis, 2015
Edited by R J Davey and C Page

First published in Great Britain in
2015, by Dagda Publishing Ltd, Nottingham, UK

First Impression, 2015

ISBN-10: 1514216310
ISBN-13: 978-1514216316

Typeset in 14pt Minion Pro and 24pt Trebuchet MS.

Legal Notice

C.J Somersby has asserted his moral right to be recognised as the author of this work.

All rights reserved. No part of this ebook may be reproduced, stored in a retrieval system, or transmitted in any form, or by any means, electronic, mechanical, photocopying, recording or otherwise, without prior written permission from the copyright holders.

This novel is a work of fiction. The characters and events portrayed are purely the product of the author's imagination. Any relation to actual persons living or dead is purely and entirely coincidental.

Dagda Publishing Ltd
62 Godfrey Street, Nottingham, NG4 2JG
Company Number: 9073900, Registered in the UK
dagdapublishing.co.uk
facebook.com/dagdapublishing
twitter.com/dagdapublishing

All enquiries: info@dagdapublishing.co.uk

For my parents, who always believed in my ability to write.
And to Roz, for her constant love and support.

"He is happy whom the Muses love. For though a man has sorrow and grief in his soul, yet when the servant of the Muses sings, at once he forgets his dark thoughts and remembers not his troubles. Such is the holy gift of the Muses to men."

~ Hesiod

Contents

Chapter 1   9
Chapter 2   15
Chapter 3   25
Chapter 4   34
Chapter 5   41
Chapter 6   45
Chapter 7   56
Chapter 8   68
Chapter 9   86
Chapter 10   103
Chapter 11   114
Chapter 12   121
Chapter 13   131
Chapter 14   136
Chapter 15   144
Chapter 16   156
Chapter 17   162
Chapter 18   173
Chapter 19   177
Chapter 20   187

Chapter 1

It was late in the afternoon when I pulled the beaten-up saloon onto the curve and shut off the engine. I sat for a moment, listening to the bodywork cooling and ignoring the growing patch of rust on the driver's door. I looked out through the window to the other side of the street. The Chicago sun was setting behind the decrepit exterior of the Schulze Baking Company Plant, casting a looming shadow across the much smaller industrial units at the intersection of Garfield & Wabash. I sighed, reached for the fedora on the passenger seat and opened the door, stepping out into the afternoon heat of the early summer.

My name is Samuel. I hate that name. My wife called me nothing else until she called me 'Defendant in the divorce'. She cited 'irreconcilable differences'. The truth is that she got tired of dealing with my curse. As far as I care, she took that name with her. I always preferred Sam as a name; it was uncomplicated.

I live in Chicago. I'm a private 'detective' – a term I use with increasing humour. I spend most of my time tracking down alimony dodgers and serving court papers. The former was why I was in this run-down area of the Windy City, standing in the fading shadow of the former prosperity that summed up the Schulze building.

It was a huge structure, dwarfing everything around it on the corner of East Garfield Boulevard. Its windows were boarded with plywood. A covered walkway skirted its first storey to protect passers-by from falling debris. One wall was supported by worn wooden beams. Fly posters lined the ageing bricks, advertising everything, from debauched club nights to third party candidates for the upcoming Presidential elections. It was a decrepit, slumbering giant; a monument to better, bygone days of the Washington Park neighbourhood. Standing there in the empty road and looking up at its fading façade, I felt an affinity I could not quite describe. My life had never exactly been a bed of roses and I had very few 'good old days' to reminisce about. Nonetheless, it definitely stirred something deeply emotional that I chose to ignore as I walked towards the building and looked for an entrance.

I had a pretty good tip that Warren James was inside. He had been moving locations for the better part of a month, deftly avoiding the authorities after skipping his court date. His wife – my client - claimed that she had gotten tired of the police's lack of priority in finding the deadbeat and had hired me to track him down. My job was to verify his location, call my client, and she would direct the boys in blue to pick him up on the basis of an 'anonymous tip.' I would pocket five hundred bucks for the privilege. It seemed an odd way of doing things, but the cash was attractive and work was sparse.

I slipped under the cover of the walkway and found what looked like an old service entrance. I paused, gently gripping the door handle, and took an optimistic moment to close my eyes and concentrate.

Nothing happened; my curse never kicked in when I wanted it to, but it was worth a try. Generally it came in fits and starts that knocked me breathless for minutes at a time. It would have to be the old-fashioned way, as usual, I thought with a grimace. I tried the door; it was unlocked and swung open a few inches. It looked like it had been forced already. Jackpot; I slipped inside. The door closed gently behind me.

The interior was gloomy and cavernous. The few windows not boarded up were filthy and the waning daylight found forcing entry to the building much more difficult than I had. Water dripped from somewhere, disturbingly loud in the silence. I stood quietly for a moment as my eyes adjusted to the gloom. Most of the equipment had been removed, but rows of conveyer belts and ovens the size of wardrobes stood abandoned and dilapidated at various points around the factory floor. Aside from the squeak of rodents fleeing the intrusion, I heard nothing to suggest that I had company. Quashing a basic urge to get back out into the fresh air, I moved further into the factory and tried not to let my footsteps echo.

I found the empty sleeping bag nestled between two rows of ovens. Food cans and beer bottles were strewn around and the stale smell of urine from a nearby wall added to the crude sense of long-term residence. I knelt down on my haunches over the sleeping bag and looked around, chewing my lip in thought. The bag could have belonged to any one of Chicago's homeless; I would need more than that to make the call to my client.

An expensive-looking shoulder bag was stuffed under a nearby conveyor, suggesting somebody who had only recently joined the streets. I shuffled across to the conveyor on my hands and knees and pulled the bag from underneath. I reached for the zipper and hesitated; I was not a police officer and I had no warrant, so this was all very illegal of me. Nonetheless, I reflected with grim logic, I had already broken a couple of laws by trespassing on private property with a loaded firearm. What could I say? Times were hard.

I pulled open the zipper and thumbed through the possessions inside; clothing, an expensive-looking music player and a wallet stuffed with dollar bills of low denominations. A driver's licence confirmed the ugly-looking man in the picture as Warren James. Bingo. I smiled victoriously, stuffed the wallet back into the bag and redid the zip quietly. I had a cell phone in my car; I would call the client from there. I stood up as silently as I could and turned to head back towards the door.

Warren James was in the doorway, a fast-food burger in one hand whilst he fumbled with a torch in the other. He must have slipped in quietly whilst my back was turned; had I a moment to react, I would have kicked myself for my lack of awareness. For a moment we just stared at each other. Then, Warren dropped the burger to the floor and I felt a brief wave of dizziness surge through my body. I threw myself behind a row of ovens just as he drew a handgun and fired it in my direction, the shot echoing like thunder through the empty factory.

I hit the ground with a grunt, sharp pain rolling up my left arm. Ignoring the agony, I scrabbled my way along the line of ovens on all fours as quickly as I could. I heard Warren's footsteps echoing like hammer strikes as he ran towards my previous position; he wanted to get his stuff back and silence me in the process. Despite the primal fear coursing through my veins, my logical side was astounded at his actions. Nobody was dumb enough to try and kill someone over a bag of clothes and an alimony cheque, I thought incredulously. As I half-ran, half-crawled from the gun-toting fugitive somewhere behind me, I started to get the sinking feeling that there were a few things my client had neglected to mention about Warren James' reasons for fleeing his marital home. I dove around the corner of the last oven in the row and pressed my back against its side, breathing hard in the darkness and trying to work out a route back to the doorway. Then the dizziness hit me again like a blow to the back of the head and my Second Sight kicked in.

That is what I call my curse. It affects me in two different ways; sometimes it exhibits a kind of 'foresight', or precognition, of things about to happen. I knew Warren was going for a gun before he even went to draw. It brings on a brief wave of nausea; nothing I can't handle. This second way only worked when physically nearby an object or person on which I was very focused – like when they are trying to kill me. Its effects are much more unpleasant.

Despite having my own tightly closed, I could see through Warren's eyes. I could hear his rapid breathing in my ears and feel the sweat on his fingers as he gripped the gun tightly. If I opened my own eyes, Warren's point of view layered over mine in the most dizzying of ways. My stomach lurched and I forced myself to keep my eyes closed, concentrating on slowing my breathing and paying attention to what my Second Sight was telling me.

I could see that he was walking slowly down the line of ovens, glancing furtively in all directions, unaware that I was right around the next corner. He jerked the gun from one direction to the other with little effort to aim; he had only been in the dark for a few moments and his eyesight had probably not yet fully adjusted. I still had a chance to get out of this.

Warren was getting closer to the edge of the oven row. Eyes still closed, I reached for my gun and hesitated. I was already deep in murky legal territory; a shoot-out with a fugitive whilst trespassing would not look good to the police officers that may already be on their way after that gunshot. I risked opening one eye to look around, holding back the wave of nausea and dissonance that came with it. A discarded piece of metal piping lay on the floor to my right; I reached out and grabbed it. The pipe scraped the concrete floor as I lifted it and I physically stopped myself from cursing at my lack of stealth. In my mind's eye I saw Warren suddenly slow as he neared the corner of the oven. He must have heard. I felt his trigger finger tensing. I felt him prepare to jump out at me.

I swung out from the corner low and hit Warren in the kneecap with the pipe. He let out a howl and dropped to one knee. I heard the handgun clatter into the darkness somewhere. Before Warren could react, I hauled myself to my feet, swivelled on one heel and punched him square in the jaw. He went over like a sack of potatoes and lay motionless on the floor, breathing steadily.

I staggered, the adrenaline leaving my system in a rush as I was reminded of the exhausting toll that my Second Sight took. I grabbed one edge of the oven block and leaned there for a few moments, concentrating on my breathing and trying not to faint. It took a few moments until I could open my eyes again. I checked the swelling bruise on my left arm and turned slowly, starting to make my way to the door. I had no idea what Warren had done, but I hardly cared by that point. I would call the client, collect my money and hand this off to someone else to deal with.

I always preferred Sam as a name; it was uncomplicated. Unfortunately, I was not.

Chapter 2

It was a couple of hours later when I arrived back at my office. My client had been thrilled at my discovery of her wayward husband; the beaming smile on her face when we met after my telephone call was a little disturbing. I comforted myself that it was nothing to do with me and pocketed the fifty-dollar bills in which she paid me. I find that money always takes the sting off a moral issue, particularly when the rent is late.

It was growing dark by the time I pulled the old Lincoln Town Car onto the curb outside my office. The sun was almost set, now just a fiery haze on the horizon. My office was on the corner of the street facing west; I was thus given a panoramic view of the horizon set ablaze, as if a great war was raging in the distance. I walked up to my door and stepped through, locking it gratefully behind me.

My office mostly comprises a single, open-plan room, with a door at the back leading off to a bathroom. It was once a storefront of some kind and still had large glass windows set along two of the walls. I had covered most of them with plywood and left a few of the smaller ones to provide light during the day. Call me a little paranoid, but I felt like a fish in a bowl until I did that. The covered windows made it refreshingly cool inside and, for a moment, I savoured the change in temperature. Flicking on the lights revealed the mess I had left from earlier that day; disposable coffee cups lined my desk and unfiled papers were strewn across the little table and sofa set that I kept in the middle of the room. It looked like a place more lived in than used for business; I winced when I realised that was true.

I picked up the few pieces of mail on my doorstep, dumped my coat onto the sofa as I passed and emptied the contents of my pockets onto the desk. I removed my gun from its holster beneath my arm and went to lock it in my desk drawer. I hesitated, looked up at my front door, and decided to leave it on the desk. I had been the victim of a few burglaries in the last couple of months and I was feeling a little jumpy. I did however lock my client's payment away in the little safe underneath my desk, making a mental note to deposit it all tomorrow and fire off a cheque to my landlord. That being settled, I walked across to one of the sofas and draped myself across it with a total lack of grace. A quick perusal of my mail found nothing interesting; a final reminder for a utilities bill that I threw to one side, a subscription offer for a private detective trade magazine and a couple of pamphlets from a major political party about why I should re-elect the 'Smith-Bowman' ticket in next year's Presidential election. Throwing it all to one side, I put both hands behind the back of my head and closed my eyes in contemplation.

My life was mostly dull. I did not mind this fact. Compared to the majority of my life, things were much better than they had been in a long while. Between the orphanage, the awful foster homes, the appearance of my Second Sight and the near-literal witch hunts it had brought upon me, this particular chapter of my existence was not so bad. And yet occasionally, I had that feeling in the pit of my stomach, the same one when I saw the crumbling façade of the Schulze plant. A feeling that something was…

"Ahem."

I sprung bolt-upright from the sofa, heart pounding like a jackhammer, and stared in astonishment at the intruder. He was six feet tall with cropped, blonde hair. He was also standing in the middle of my office and watching me. Something in the movement of his eyes reminded me of a cat watching a mouse. He was dressed in a suit of grey charcoal and wore a dark blue tie. He had both hands clasped together in front of his jacket and stood motionless, as if waiting for something to happen. When I simply continued to gape at him, he cleared his throat again and asked, in a gently enquiring tone, "Samuel Black?"

I opened my mouth and closed it again. He stood looking at me with the patience of a boulder. My eyes flicked to the locked front door and then briefly around the room, trying to work out where he had come from. There were no other entrances. The windows not already boarded did not open. There was nowhere that he could have hidden.

He sighed, a small expression that somehow came across as aloof. My astonishment quickly changed to irritation as he glanced around my office, surveying what he saw with an air of implied distaste. He seemed less than impressed by my current state of life, and this judgement annoyed me. So I folded my arms across my chest, took a minute step closer to my desk, where my gun still lay, and raised my chin slightly before I spoke. "Yeah, that's me," I said. "And who the hell are you?"

He flinched at the expletive and a little corner of my brain jeered in victory at his discomfort. He took a breath and exhaled slowly; not quite a sigh, more like he was preparing for an uncomfortable conversation. "My name is Alleam," he said slowly, weighing and assessing each word for accuracy and effect. "And I need your help."

The inquisitive part of me was instantly intrigued, but the majority of my brain was still gibbering at how this man had simply managed to appear. "How did you..?" I asked finally, gesturing at the door.

Alleam ignored my question, which irritated me more. "Samuel, it's important that you listen to me," he said in the same calm, careful manner as before. "I have very little time to explain what I need from you. There are hostile elements trying to locate us as we speak."

Jesus, I thought; this guy was either crazy or dangerous. I edged a little closer to my desk, trying to make it look like I was simply adjusting my stance. "Look, Al," I said, feeling another little moment of glee at how the abbreviation brought an irritated flicker to his face. "I'm all up for this cloak and dagger stuff; it's all very exciting. However, I'm going to need you to answer a few questions before we can-" I cut off in mid-sentence, turned and launched myself towards my gun, hoping to take him by surprise.

The wave of heat hit me in the side and knocked me clean across the room, slamming me head-first into a filing cabinet. I hit the floor and lay there for a moment, dazed and thoroughly confused at what had just happened. My hand stung sharply, and I looked down to find it had reddened like bad sunburn. I looked up at Alleam and my breath caught in my throat.

He was standing in the middle of the room as before, one hand raised. He was surrounded by a near-dazzling glow of blue-white energy, as if his very aura had been set alight. His eyes were shining bright blue and his lips were twisted in a grimace that was aimed directly at me. After a moment, the glow in his eyes faded and the halo of light disappeared. He lowered his hand slowly and surveyed me with a look that bordered on impatience.

I pushed myself to my feet, suddenly feeling scared and very vulnerable. The gun was still lying on my desk but by this point I hardly dared to move. I just stood, gaping open-mouthed at Alleam with a million questions rushing through my head. Eventually I found my voice and shakily asked, "What the hell are you?"

Alleam stared at me for a long moment, ignoring the expletive. "I'm an angel," he said simply. "And you're going to help me stop the Apocalypse."

If I had been in any other situation, I would have thought

Alleam was delusional. In this case, I found him delusional and terrifying.

He stood there, simply watching me for a reaction. A clock ticked slowly on the wall, a reminder that only seconds had passed since his audacious statement, stated as calmly and factually as if commenting on the weather.

I just stared at him. The logical part of my brain was working overtime. He had to be insane; delusional certainly. And yet, I had been thrown across the room without being touched, and the burn on my hand just completely defied anything rational. So, with no other idea on what to do, I simply said as politely as possible, "Excuse me?"

Alleam gave another little sigh and shook his head in a resigned way. "It always amazes me how the inhabitants of this world can avoid the truth," he said wearily. "They believe in a deity that has not directly interacted with them for thousands of years. And yet, when something appears directly in front of their eyes they simply refuse to accept it as fact." He turned to look out a window and for a moment I saw sadness in his eyes. "We are all running out of time," he said, staring at the fiery horizon of the setting sun. "And if I had anywhere else to turn…" Alleam suddenly straightened and turned back to look at me, determination in his eyes. "I need you, Samuel," he said.

I swallowed, trying to rationalise what I was experiencing and failing miserably. "Let's assume for a moment that you're telling the truth," I said in the most even tone I could make through my tightened vocal chords. "What could I possibly do to help you?"

Alleam cocked his head slightly, studying me for a moment. "I need your Sight," he said.

By this point, every mental alarm bell I possessed was ringing at full volume. I felt my palms getting sweaty. "H-how do you know about that?" I asked shakily, half-hoping that he would not answer.

He did not, simply standing there and staring at me. I got the impression that he was losing patience. "You have a gift that very few others do, Samuel," he said pointedly. "You have an ability to see things that others cannot; you have a gift of gaining information, and I need that gift." He licked his lips briefly. "The Horsemen of the Apocalypse have been loosed upon this world, and I need to find them."

Horsemen of the Apocalypse; this guy was deadly serious about what he was saying. I was getting dangerously close to losing the plot entirely, so I moved slowly towards the sofa before my knees buckled. Alleam watched me move but did not try to stop me. I sat down gently and took a couple of deep breaths. I needed to ground this all in something familiar before I lost what little remained of my sense of reality. "Okay," I said after a moment, breathing slowly. "What you're saying is, you need me to use my…" I hesitated briefly. "…particular investigative talents to get information on a person you are trying to find?"

I saw irritation flash across Alleam's eyes again and he opened his mouth as if to rebuke me. After a moment, he thought better of it and stayed silent. Perhaps he had finally realised that the impact of the information dump he was putting on me and thought it was best for my sanity to back off a little. "Essentially, at this stage, yes," he said after a moment.

I took a deep breath, grateful for this small consideration. "So, in order to find information on this…person you are looking for," I said carefully, refusing point-blank to use the word 'Horseman', "I need an idea on where to start looking."

Alleam smiled. He reached into his suit jacket; I flinched, but all he produced was a brown envelope. He slit the seal with one pale finger and emptied the contents onto the table. There were a number of photographs, several of which depicted a compound of some kind. It was surrounded by high, barbed wire-topped walls, but the photographer's vantage point allowed a view into the courtyard. A series of buildings were arrayed around the edges of the compound whilst a large group of motorcycles were parked along the concrete. Some photos were much more closely-zoomed; I could see the faces of people in leather jackets walking to and fro. I squinted a little, sifting through the photos with one hand. "A biker compound," I remarked. "I don't recognise these group markings. Who are they?"

Alleam looked down from over my shoulder with a dispassionate expression. "They are also angels," he said. "They are here to oversee the end of your world and to co-ordinate with the Horsemen in their tasks."

I laughed out loud; by that point, it was either laugh or start screaming. I turned to look up at Alleam. "You seriously expect me to believe that just because you throw together some kind of…" I gestured fitfully at him and towards the area that I had been thrown by the earlier blast wave "…special effects show that I will swallow this crap about angels and the end of the world?" I stood, face-to-face now with him, anger rising in my chest. "I don't know who the hell you are or how you're able to do what you do, but if you think I'm stupid enough to-"

I was suddenly three inches in the air and could not breathe. Alleam was staring at me with a hard look in his eyes. He had not moved a muscle and yet I felt his hands invisibly around my throat, lifting me from the ground effortlessly. "I have very little patience for your disrespect, Samuel," he said in a steely tone. "And I am risking my own exposure by indulging in these little demonstrations to show you just how deadly serious I am." He let me go and I staggered as I hit the floor, collapsing onto the couch and heaving for breath. Alleam ignored my retching and leant over, picking up a particular photograph from the assortment on the table. "This is Banniel," he said, thrusting the picture into my grasp. "He is the senior-most figure overseeing events here on Earth. At the moment, only he knows the identity of the first Horseman to act."

I looked down dazedly at the picture in my hand, breathing heavily as I recovered my oxygen levels. A tall, stern looking man with short, dark hair and a chiselled jaw stared somewhere off-camera with a brooding expression. The breast pocket patch of his leather jacket said 'President' in bold, capital letters. I opened my mouth to retort something but the logical part of my brain kicked in fast enough to silence the wisecrack before I made it. I did not want a repeat of the last few moments. "And what do you expect me to do?" I asked, my voice still rasping a little from the pressure to my throat.

Alleam smiled a little. "Use your gift, Samuel; that is all. Use it to spy on him and find out the identity I need. I will deal with the rest." He fished into another pocket and pulled out a second envelope. "We have a contact on the inside; a Sister of the holy orders. She will help you to get close to Banniel." He held out the envelope to me. I took it hesitantly; it was surprisingly heavy. "There is a picture of her in there, along with currency for our services," Alleam continued. "I understand that you have…material concerns here in this world," and he glanced pointedly at the calendar on my wall where I had marked my overdue rent. "I have access to the resources to employ your services for as long as needed," he said matter-of-factly.

I opened the envelope. A thick wad of hundred-dollar bills were packed inside. I swallowed again, trying to reconcile the terror of this conversation with the pleasure of seeing so much money. Alongside the cash there was a picture of a very attractive lady with long, dark hair, jeans and a biker jacket. The word 'Prospect' was emblazoned across the back of it. Someone had scrawled her name in pen at the bottom of the photo; Miriam. "How do I contact her?" I asked, studying the face in the picture with a little more than professional interest.

"Through myself," Alleam replied, reaching into another pocket and dropping something onto the table. It was a business card, almost entirely blank except for a telephone number across one side. "When you are ready to meet her, contact me and I will arrange the details," he said. Then he looked me square in the eye. "I would suggest that you do not take too long," he added in a stern tone.

I swallowed again at the implied threat, nodded and looked back down at the photograph. "This is going to be a pretty hard infiltration with no back-up," I said aloud, half-thinking to myself as I looked down at the picture in my hands and then to the others spread across the desk.

"Don't worry; I've taken care of that, too." Alleam said, his voice suddenly sounding much more distant. I looked up to ask him exactly what he meant and found myself alone in the room. The office door was still locked.

I slumped down onto the sofa, confused and hurting. For a moment I earnestly believed that I had been hallucinating, but the pictures spread across the table and the hundreds of dollars in their neat little envelope put an end to that delusion. I leant forward, stared down at the photographs and the money on the table, and thought hard.

I had no idea what had just happened and no way to explain what I had just experienced. Alleam – whoever he was – seemed to have some kind of ability to manipulate his environment and other people without physically touching someone. That was terrifying, but not unbelievable; given my own unusual gift of perception, I had always been open-minded to others existing with extraordinary gifts. But his claims of angelhood and declarations about the Horsemen of the Apocalypse seemed more suited to street corner extremists with cardboard signs. I kept staring down at the photos of the bikers, the back of their leather jackets depicting a pair of folded wings. Embossed over the wings was their gang name. 'Angeles de la Muerte'; The Angels of Death.

It felt like my sanity was unwinding again, so I tried to look at the whole situation as rationally as I could; someone had just given me a lot of money to find information on a person they were trying to track down; nothing more, nothing less. It soothed my mind to place the whole thing in a rational setting; just another client, just another job. Follow your normal routine and you will get out of this in one piece.

Or at least, I mused as I stared down at the photos of the biker gang, my injuries from Alleam's paranormal demonstrations still stinging on my skin, in as few pieces as I could manage.

Chapter 3

The Angeles de la Muerte's compound was an hour's drive south of Chicago, just off Interstate 57. It was accessible only by a single lane track from the main roadway and looked like it had once been a warehouse complex for container trucks. The large, imposing walls around the sides of the complex prevented prying eyes from seeing into the daily life of the biker gang; only the tops of the largest warehouse buildings could be seen peeking over the barbed wire that adorned them.

It was early morning, only ten or eleven hours since Alleam's visit. I had spent the rest of the evening trying to pull together what little information I could find on the Angeles de la Muerte and being surprised at how little there was. Biker gangs large enough to buy their own compounds tended to have turned up in the public eye at some point, even for completely harmless reasons. It was as if this group had just appeared overnight, moved in quietly and set up shop with as little fanfare as they could achieve. I doubted if their neighbours in the village of Monee, only a few miles south, knew they were even there.

I had then tried to sleep but found myself staring at the ceiling, mind racing uncontrollably. I just could not comprehend what I had been through in the past twelve hours. Alleam obviously had some paranormal talents; in a way, that was oddly relieving. I had never come across anyone else who had the ability to do something so completely logic-defying. I found myself feeling elated; happy that I was not the only person out there with bizarre abilities.

What worried me was Alleam's complete conviction to the extreme religious statements he had made about his origin and purpose. I rationalised that it was entirely possible for someone with his power to develop delusions of holiness as an explanation for his predicament. Odds were that his issues with the biker gang were completely terrestrial in origin. But his declarations of Apocalypse and angels continued to ring in my ears and scared me more than I wanted to admit.

Unable to sleep more than a few hours, I had decided to face the situation sooner than later. I was working with a lot of speculation and very little information; something I hated doing. Firstly, I had rang and left a message for Jim O'Donald, a detective contact of mine over at Chicago Police. Jim and I had been professional acquaintances for a number of years and we had helped each other out with information on several occasions. The desk Sergeant at police headquarters had agreed to leave a message for Jim to call me when he arrived for his shift. Then I had picked up Alleam's card and dialled the number. It rang twice before it picked up, and an androgynous voice I did not recognise answered. "Two hours from now; she will be waiting. Don't look suspicious", the voice said bluntly. Then the voice gave me an address for the compound and hung up abruptly.

That had been almost two hours ago. I had packed a few things I thought may be useful and driven the Lincoln down to meet my contact and see the place first-hand. I had pulled up on South Ridgeland Avenue a short distance down from the compound. I knew practically nothing about this biker gang or how private they were about their business so I decided to avoid pulling up directly opposite the compound, just in case some paranoid look-out with authority issues decided to take a pot shot at an unrecognised onlooker. The voice on the telephone had told me not to look suspicious so I popped the hood of the Lincoln and rolled up the sleeves of my jacket, leaning over the engine block and pretending to fix some imaginary fault.

The sun had risen a couple of hours earlier and I was

bathed in the warm morning light as I waited. Ploughed fields of brown and green hues stretched out to either side of me. Birds chirped nearby in the cluster of trees that lined the compound's access track. It was deceptively peaceful and extremely private, perhaps exactly the reason why the bikers had chosen this location.

Observing the compound, my feelings of peace rapidly disappeared. The tall, foreboding walls gave an unwelcoming impression, and I saw the occasional gang member patrolling the outside perimeter like soldiers keeping guard. I was unable to discern any weapons but I was certain they were armed. My gut clenched with nerves and I took a couple of deep breaths.

I had been there around fifteen minutes. I was just starting to worry about how long I could linger without looking suspicious when I saw the massive front gates swing open. A beige panel van with tinted windows pulled out onto the access track and proceeded up to the tree-lined junction with the road. It turned in my direction and pulled up on the opposite side of the road from me, engine still running.

The driver's door opened and a woman stepped down onto the road. To say she was exactly like her photograph would be an injustice; she was even more beautiful in person. Long, dark hair flowed down over the back of her biker jacket and her bright blue eyes contrasted sharply against both her hair colour and pale skin. She wore tight fitting jeans and a non-descript black T-shirt that hugged her at the waist and the chest. Despite the danger of the situation, I found myself gawping.

She looked either way along the road and crossed to me. Her eyes locked with mine and I saw caution in her gaze. "Having trouble, friend?" she enquired, a little too loudly for normal conversation.

I glanced at the van. Through the door, I could see another person sitting in the passenger seat; a man in biker leathers with a Prospect's patch as well. I looked back at the lady and smiled, replying as casually as I could. "Yeah, can't get it to start. Could you take a look?"

She smiled broadly; I saw some trembling at the corner of her mouth. "Well, I normally do bikes, but I can take a look. Anything I don't know about engines, I'm sure my friend can help." And she nodded at her companion in the van.

I turned to look at the other Prospect and smiled politely in his direction, nodding in appreciation at the implied assistance. He just stared at me with an emotionless face. I kept smiling, turning away to lean back over the engine block. "Are you Miriam?" I asked in a low voice.

"Not here!" she hissed, which I took to be a confirmation. She reached into the engine and proceeded to unhook and reattach a few hose clips, making it look like she was searching for a fault. "I've been pulled out to do some club business; we'll have to talk another time." Louder, she said, "I think it's an electrical connection," for the attention of her stone-faced companion.

I nodded, reaching out and idly fiddling with a few wires to make it seem like we were both working. "Just tell me when and where," I said, glancing at her face from the corner of my eye.

She chewed momentarily on her lower lip, a little nervous action that belied her calm exterior. "I will be out on club errands all of tomorrow; I should be able to shake my escort for a little while." She glanced up at me. "The telephone number you called today will contact you with a time and a place." Then she stood up from the engine, fixed me with a wide, false grin and said, "Try it now."

I complied, reaching through the open driver's window and tried the ignition. Naturally, the car roared into life and I pantomimed gratitude. "Thank you, you're very kind," I said to her.

Miriam nodded in response. "Not a problem," she said cheerfully, although the look in her eyes betrayed her. She was terrified. "Safe journey friend," she added.

I smiled, reached one hand to my head and tapped my temple in an informal salute. "You too," I replied. I also turned to nod politely again at the biker in the van. He ignored me. Miriam climbed back into the driver's seat and closed the door. A moment later the van rolled away towards Chicago.

I watched the van for a few moments, pondering my first meeting with Miriam. She was brave, I gave her that. I wondered how she had ended up involved with the bikers in the first place; Alleam had claimed that she was a 'sister of the holy orders', which seemed rather fitting with the rest of his religious declarations. I sighed, not sure what to make of the whole situation, and turned to get back into the Lincoln.

I had been so preoccupied that I had somehow not noticed the police cruiser crawling to a halt behind me. It bore the dark blue and white colours of the Monee Police Department, the local law enforcement in this area outside of Chicago. Two officers climbed out of the front seats and started towards me. The driver was a woman, tall with short, blonde hair and a stern expression. Her companion was a male, slightly shorter with dark hair and a thick, bristling moustache. Both wore large pairs of aviator sunglasses that hid their eyes.

I smiled and clasped both hands together in front of my waist, trying to look as unthreatening as possible. "Good morning, officers," I said as cheerfully as I could. I glanced at the compound. The guards were still there but they had slowed their pace to watch what was happening. I tried to keep as calm as possible; one wrong move could definitely end up with someone getting shot. So I continued to grin broadly at both officers. "How can I help you today?" I asked.

The female officer gave a cursory glance at my old Lincoln before looking me up and down and wrinkling her nose in distaste. I felt uncomfortable and a little irritated; I was not exactly dressed to impress but I hardly looked unkempt. Then she looked me in the eye for a long moment. "We had some reports of a disturbance out here," she said, resting one hand on her equipment belt. The catch on her holster was unbuttoned and I could see the matte grey butt of a police issue taser resting menacingly within. A handgun was holstered on her other hip. She was unnervingly well-armed. "We thought we should come check things out," she continued.

I continued to smile, being very careful not to make any sudden movements. There was something about this whole situation that made me uneasy but I could not quite touch on why. The cops were behaving a little oddly, even for a profession that allowed quite a power trip for the egotistical. "I'm just out for a morning drive, officer," I said with forced pleasantry. "Ran into a little engine trouble, but a kind Samaritan helped me get it fixed." I glanced down the road back towards Chicago. "I was just about to move on."

"Uh-huh," the officer said. She glanced over at my car again. "You wouldn't mind if we took a look inside your vehicle, would you sir?" she said with a pointed sneer.

I gritted my teeth, pretended I was grinning and shook my head. "Be my guest, officer," I said.

She smirked, and turned to her partner. "Check inside," she ordered. As her companion flung open the driver's side door with little concern for its hinges, she turned back to me. "You'll have to wait on the side of the road," she said bluntly, jerking her head towards the cornfield beyond the road's shoulder.

I sighed, raised both hands in an expression of submission and then turned my back on her.

Almost instantly I felt a wave of dizziness surge through my body. Acting on instinct, I threw myself to one side just as she fired the taser at my back. I hit the ground with a grunt and rolled quickly behind my car, crouching against the rear bumper. I heard a curse and then footsteps on concrete as she rounded the corner of the vehicle. I threw myself forward at waist height and caught her just as she appeared at the tail light, sending her sprawling backwards onto the road. Her taser went flying from her grip, clattering away along the road. Her glasses had been knocked off in the scuffle and I found myself staring into her eyes.

They were a glowing, fiery red that burned into my retinas like an open flame. I yelped in pain and was thrown off in my moment of disorientation. I landed on my back, winded, with the two police officers standing over me. The woman snarled at me before going to retrieve her weapon. Her partner, still wearing his sunglasses, towered over me. He unholstered his own taser and pointed it down at my chest.

I could hear shouts of alarm from the biker's compound. A klaxon started wailing. Both officers looked up in alarm as the front gates to the compound began winding open again. The sounds of motorcycles revving could be heard and the guards on the perimeter were now running in our direction. The male officer swore in a language I did not understand, looked back down at me along the sights of the taser and went to pull the trigger.

There was a noise like a thunderclap. From nowhere, a white-blue streak of light came barrelling towards us. The male officer turned to react but barely had time to raise his arms before he was knocked sideways by the mass of light. Whatever it was, it blasted out across the field before turning and heading back towards us.

From the corner of my eye, I saw the female officer grab

the fallen taser, her head moving rapidly in all directions to locate the assailant. The compound guards were getting closer and the first few motorcycles were appearing at the front gates. She howled in frustration and, in the blink of an eye, simply vanished. Her partner struggled to his feet, glared at me from above his sunglasses with red, fiery eyes similar to his partner, and also vanished. I was suddenly alone, dazed and hurt, being closed upon by an entire gang of bikers.

Things were not going according to plan.

The blue light was now moving towards me at enormous speed, showing no signs of stopping. Before I could move or cry out, the light crashed into me with a roar of noise and engulfed my body. Everything went white. I blinked…

…and found myself outside my office in west Chicago. My car was sitting slightly askew in the parking lane, the driver's side door still open from where the male police officer – or whatever he actually was - had been rooting around inside. My head swam with disorientation and I fell to one knee on the sidewalk. "How…?" I muttered to myself dazedly.

A pair of hands reached out; I took them and was hauled to my feet. I staggered, still dizzy from the fight and my inexplicable relocation. I felt the pair of hands catch me under the arms and I looked up into the crystal blue eyes of a tall, white-haired young lady in a charcoal grey suit. She looked down at me with what seemed like concern and helped me regain my balance. "Are you okay?" she asked.

I nodded and she let go, allowing me to stand unaided. "Yes, thank you," I said, shaking my head in confusion. "I just had the strangest thing happe-" I cut off in mid-sentence, staring at her hands. They were surrounded in an aura of white-blue light, fading now. The exact colour of the light I had seen attack the police offers.

The exact same colour, I suddenly realised, of the aura I

had seen around Alleam.

I took a step back, suddenly very afraid. "Who are you?" I demanded.

The woman stared at me, her gaze steady and completely calm. "My name is Anahita," she said. Then she bowed her head formally before adding, "I'm your guardian angel."

Chapter 4

"Let me get this straight; you're my what?"

We were inside my office, and I was still as dazed as I had been outside. Anahita had simply picked me up as easily as a she would a small child and carried me quite literally through my locked front door, before placing me gently on the couch. I had just lain there with my eyes closed whilst I waited for my head to stop spinning, savouring the cool, darkened air of my office and forcing myself to think of little else. After about ten minutes, I opened my eyes again and turned my head gently to see Anahita perched uneasily on the opposite couch like a nervous house guest. She was watching me intently, her eyes full of caution. She pursed her lips briefly in response to my question. "I'm your guardian angel," she repeated, her eyes never leaving mine.

I pushed myself up into a seated position, groaning as my head started to swim again. "Okay," I said to myself, trying to think clearly. "And you were the one who saved me from…?" I trailed off, unable to adequately describe what had happened less than an hour before, so I simply gestured towards the front door.

Anahita nodded; her startlingly clear, blue eyes were still fixed on my face. "That's right," she said quietly.

I nodded slowly, the full weight of the day's events beginning to sink in. "So he was telling the truth," I said to myself, before looking back to Anahita quite suddenly. She visibly flinched; I was struck by the level of caution she was expressing towards me and filed it away for future query. "What Alleam said earlier," I clarified. "Angels are real."

Anahita nodded. "Yes," she said.

I sat silent for a moment, contemplating my feet. "And the Apocalypse?" I asked, fearing the answer.

Anahita pursed her lips again; a nervous gesture, it seemed. "Beginning to unfold as we speak," she confirmed.

I laughed; it was the only thing I could think of doing. My head was spinning again but I forced myself off the chair, in dire need of a drink. I could feel Anahita's eyes on the back of my head as I moved across to a filing cabinet and pulled open the top drawer. An absence of files was made up for by a large bottle of cheap whisky; I pulled the stopper and took a short slug. "Those cops weren't human, were they?" I asked quietly, my eyes fixed on the wall in front of me. "What were they?"

I heard Anahita take a small, hesitant intake of breath. "I can't tell you that," she said.

I turned back to her, whisky bottle still in one hand, my eyes full of exasperation and sudden anger. "You can't tell me?" I exclaimed, taking a few steps towards the couch. Anahita eyed me warily and despite my anger I was struck once again by how cautious she seemed to be about me. I started counting off events on the fingers of my free hand. "In the past twenty-four hours I have been attacked by a literal angel," I began, "I've been roped into some hare-brained scheme about stopping the Apocalypse by spying on another angel and nearly tasered by monsters disguised as cops." I stared at Anahita with frustration. "And that was before you showed up and performed your little teleportation trick on me," I said, swallowing a large shot of liquor in a bid to calm my heart-rate.

Anahita just sat there, looking at me silently. "A trick that saved your life," she observed in that same quiet, cautious tone.

I was stopped in my tracks, unable to think of a retort. My shoulders slumped, the anger rushing out of my body to be replaced with utter, wearied confusion. I slumped down onto the couch and gently placed the whisky bottle on the table before resting my face in my hands. She was right; she had saved my life. Whatever those things were, they had been gunning for me in the most unpleasant of ways. Anahita had blown through them like a literal force of nature and had rescued me from the clutches of both monster and biker gang. In truth, I was not really angry at her; I was just terrified. It seemed that everything Alleam had said – all his seemingly ridiculous and delusional statements about angels and the end of the world – was rapidly being proven by the day's events. That scared me more than anything. I looked up to see Anahita still staring at me, hardly having moved a muscle. "I'm sorry," I said quietly. "You did save my life, and I thank you for it."

She quirked an eyebrow, seemingly unsure on how to respond. Then she simply inclined her head in a gesture of acceptance. "I am your guardian; it is my duty," she said. "But I am just a soldier; I have no authorisation to answer your questions. Only Alleam can do that."

I nodded, rubbing my face with both palms. "Fair enough," I said, leaning back on the couch. A thought struck my mind. "Can they follow me?" I asked. "Those monsters that tried to get me; can they follow me back here?"

Anahita shook her head. "They were long gone before I moved our location," she replied. She sounded certain and I believed her.

I nodded. "And the bikers, the…other angels," I said, eyeing Anahita for her reaction. She simply nodded a little to confirm the unasked question. "Can they find me?"

Anahita hesitated for a moment. "It seems unlikely," she said finally. "We were only there briefly when they noticed us; I don't think they would have had time to identify you or your vehicle's registration."

I grunted; it was a risk, but a moment's thought led me to agree that it was unlikely. If anyone did come knocking, I would have to rely on my Second Sight to identify any potential attacker before they struck. So I just nodded and fixed Anahita with a curious gaze. "So how does this guardian angel thing work?" I asked, resisting the urge to reach for the bottle again. Medicinal was one thing, but I needed my wits about me for the foreseeable future.

Anahita thought for a moment. "I am your physical guardian and protector," she said finally. "I act to defend you against physical threats. You can summon me with a thought when you feel you need my assistance. I am also linked with you emotionally," she continued, watching me carefully. "Essentially, I feel what you feel. In times of strong emotions related to fear about your wellbeing, I am able to materialize on my own judgement to protect you."

"Which is what you did earlier?" I asked. She nodded. I sighed, letting this information process for a moment. "Okay," I said finally, and then looked up at her again. "Again, thank-you," I said with genuine gratitude.

Anahita tilted her head again formally. "It is my role," she simply acknowledged. She then went to say something else but stopped, her head tilted a little as if listening to something beyond my hearing. Suddenly she stood. "I must go," she said hurriedly. "I am needed elsewhere." She turned towards the door before I could say anything else and then paused, looking back at me. "I am here to help," she said quietly. "Remember that." And with a brief, high-pitched note that emanated from nowhere in particular, she simply disappeared.

I was alone, sitting in the cool darkness of my office, my mind running with a million different thoughts. I groaned, leaning my head back against the cushions of the couch and trying to make some sense of the last twelve hours. The whisky had kicked in by now and had brought a certain calming effect that allowed me to think a little clearer.

It was all true; I had no basis to deny it. Alleam and Anahita, the red-eyed monsters posing as cops that had tried to taser me, the teleportation; there was no way I could explain any of that away in a logical manner. Throw in Alleam's comments about the Apocalypse and I was in way over my head. It was all I could do not to reach out for the whisky and just tip the entire bottle back in a desperate bid to escape the crushing realisations I was coming to.

The phone rang and I jumped. "Definitely getting some sleep tonight," I muttered, reaching over to the table between the couches to pick up the receiver. I paused as a thought struck me; Miriam had said that I would be contacted to arrange a further meeting. I picked up the receiver and held it to my ear, genuinely uncertain of what would happen next. "Hello?" I asked warily.

"Sam, it's me," Jim O'Donald's deep, cheerful voice resounded down the receiver. I instantly felt more relaxed at hearing my old friend's voice; Jim and I had worked together for years at opposite ends of the criminal investigation spectrum; we had bonded over many late nights featuring gruesome cases and bad beer. "Man, you sound like hell."

I laughed a little despite myself, leaning back again on the couch. "One of those days," I said, resting both feet on the table and marvelling inwardly at the level of understatement in that explanation. "You got my message?" I asked.

"Yeah," Jim replied absently. I could hear him shuffling papers on his desk. "There's not much I can give you, to be honest; even the people over at Organised Crime have got next to nothing on these guys."

I nodded to myself, unsurprised. "Alright, just give me what you've got," I said, preparing myself to take mental notes.

Jim paused for a moment before responding. "The Angeles de la Muerte; they're a biker gang that first came up on our radar about a month ago," he said. "They bought the compound through a front company that deals with parcel delivery; haven't made much noise since." I heard him shuffle papers again. "We've had no reports of criminal activity, no complaints from the general public, not even a speeding ticket." He sighed. "We were worried for a while that we may have a biker war brewing right on the eve of the visit, but it never seemed to come to anything."

"What visit?" I enquired, absently scratching one ankle with the heel of my shoe.

Jim snorted. "Geez Sam, do you even interact with modern society anymore? We've got both the President and the Vice-President flying in over the next few days as part of the campaign tour."

"Oh yeah, that." I said, glancing over at the discarded campaign literature I had been sent in the post yesterday. Then I frowned as a thought struck me and I leant forward a little. "What made you guys think you had a biker war brewing?" I asked curiously.

"Well, another biker group moved in around the same time," Jim explained, shuffling more papers. "They were – yeah, here it is; Los Hijos de la Parias," he read out. "They were apparently setting themselves up with similar infrastructure – a compound, front company in the haulage game - so we thought there might be a turf war about to kick off. It seems that both gangs have been keeping out of the other's business though." Jim's voice took on a note of concern. "You aren't getting yourself stuck into something over your head, are you? I know what you're like, Sam."

I hesitated, wondering if I should mention the fake cops that had tried to attack me. I decided against it; whatever those monsters were, they were strong and they were dangerous. I knew barely enough to keep myself out of danger right now; getting police officers killed in a confrontation with something supernatural before I could give them more information was something I could not handle. Besides, I reasoned, they had been specifically gunning for me today so chances were that it had been a temporary disguise. So instead I put on my usual jovial tone and replied, "Don't worry buddy, I'm not stupid enough to get myself involved in biker business."

Jim sounded unconvinced. "Okay," he said finally. "But you know the drill Sam; you find anything major, you call it in." His warning tone then melted into good-natured humour. "Good hunting buddy; let me know if you need anything else."

"Thanks," I replied, and sat for a moment listening to the

dial tone after Jim hung up. I replaced the receiver and lay back on the couch, suddenly feeling very tired. Another gang in town at the same time as The Angels of Death; it could be a coincidence but years of detective work made me think it unlikely. Woozily, I tried to think back over my high school Spanish lessons. Los Hijos de la Parias translated roughly to 'The Children of the Pariah'; that did not sound good.

I tried to order my thoughts and work out what my next step should be but the exhaustion of the fight, the stresses of the unfolding revelations and the calming effect of the whisky made it impossible. I found myself drifting until I yielded to the inevitable and curled myself up onto the sofa, gratefully accepting the rushing tide of slumber.

Not stupid enough to get involved in biker business, I had said to Jim; perhaps not.

Getting involved in the business of angels; that was a whole new level of dumb.

Chapter 5

"Step this way, citizens!"

I shook my head in confusion, the unfamiliar voice ringing in my ears. The world was a wash of overlapping colours and shapes that made my stomach churn. I staggered, knocking into one of the shapes and heard it cry out in astonishment and annoyance. I fell to one knee, the shapes all around me in a swarming mass, and squeezed my eyes shut to try and regain my balance. When I opened them again, everything was in focus.

It was night and I was outside, the moon shining down on me as bright as a furnace. I was standing on the edge of a town square, the buildings all around me made of wooden beams and irregular designs. The shapes around me had coalesced into a large crowd of people, all moving in the same direction into the square. They were all dressed strangely; old-style clothes like something you would see at a 17th century historical re-enactment. I slowly pushed myself to my feet, grasping at my clothing to see if I had my gun stashed anywhere. The material felt strange, and I looked down to see that I was wearing similar style clothing to everyone around me. I opened my mouth to say something to a passer-by but then closed it again and frowned. Something was telling me to move into the square with the rest of the crowd; some little voice in my head that whispered that I had something to see. Dazed and uncertain, I fell into pace with the rest of the crowd and followed them into the square.

The crowd was huge; looming dark figures in the half-light of torches that lined the edge of the square. They were talking in hushed whispers and pointing towards the centre. I squinted at a raised wooden platform, a hooded figure standing atop its beams. The whispering voice told me to step forward and I did, pushing past the other figures in the crowd with scant concern for their mutters of annoyance. I had to see what was happening.

The hooded figure was a man bound to a giant wooden beam, his head covered with a cloth bag. Large piles of wood were piled around his legs. Occasionally he moaned and lolled his head from side to side, as if only half-awake. I stood at the front of the crowd, my mind gripped with fear as I understood what I was seeing.

Another person stepped up onto the platform. His well-fitting clothing and air of surety indicated a man of authority. He stopped at the front of the podium and raised both hands. The crowd went silent and the man began to speak. "As the duly-appointed magistrate for this area," he declared in a loud, booming voice, "we stand here to witness, having been duly tried and convicted, the punishment of a warlock."

The crowd burst into cheers and cat-calls aimed at the hooded figure. His head shook more violently, clearly distressed by the increase in noise. The magistrate raised his hands again and the noise dissipated. "I hereby sentence this abomination against mankind to burn at the stake until he is dead," he declared triumphantly. "And may God have mercy on his soul."

The crowd cheered again, louder than before. I saw the magistrate walk to one side of the platform and gesture to one of the men stood there. He held a lit torch, the light silhouetting his fanatically wide eyes as he held it out to the magistrate. The magistrate inclined his head in thanks, stepped back grandly to the centre of the podium and turned to the hooded figure. I saw him cross himself and bow his head in a short prayer, before kneeling at the foot of the prisoner and touching the torch to the wood. Within a few moments, the crackling of kindling brought renewed cheers from the crowd. I just stood there, shaking my head slowly, somehow knowing what was going to happen next. "No," I whispered.

The prisoner struggled as the fire spread rapidly, the flames biting hungrily at his feet. He struggled against his restraints and I could hear him shouting things too muffled to hear. The night sky was turning darker and a few members of the cheering crowd had stopped to look up, muttering in confusion and fear. Lightning flashed across the sky; massive, forked spikes of sheer electricity appearing out of nowhere and crashing into the ground. The crowd seemed to collectively scream as the sudden impacts shook the earth, causing several people to lose their balance and fall.

The wind suddenly picked up, increasing until a gale howled around the town square. I bowed my head and covered my face to protect my sight as people around me were knocked to the floor. Utter chaos reigned as people tried to escape in all directions. I managed to open one eye and looked up at the platform in time to see the prisoner throw back his head and loose an angry howl towards the sky, the pitch and tone echoing across the square despite the muffling effect of the bag. The burning beams at his feet came to life and shot out in all directions, a volley of fiery missiles tearing into the crowd. I saw one hit the magistrate directly in the chest and send him flying off the platform, only to be trampled by the crowd. I just stood where I was, looking up at the platform as best as I could through the howling gale of the winds. I saw the man who had handed the magistrate his torch struggling across the podium, the gusts of wind threatening to throw him into the crowd at every step. He had a knife in one hand. I watched, unable to move as the young man fought his way step-by-step to the hooded figure and, with a cry of righteous fury, stabbed the knife into his chest.

The hooded figure cried out. Almost instantly the gale disappeared and any wooden beams still in the air fell to the ground as if cut from strings. The hooded figure slumped forward against the ropes that bound him, his head lolling forward like a ragdoll.

I took a deep breath, my heart pounding. I saw the man with the knife reach up to the hood. He untied the string that held it against the prisoner's neck and loosened the opening. Then, in one quick flourish, he tore the bag from the prisoner's head and jumped back, as if scared of being bitten.

I stood there, staring at my own deceased face, and tried to scream.

Chapter 6

I woke up in a cold sweat, gasping for air. I was still on the couch in my office; from the dim light, I guessed that it was well into the evening. I must have slept most of the day. I pushed myself up into a seated position, my mind still whirling with the images of the dream. I leant forward and rubbed my face with both palms. It had been years since I had dreamt like that. For a moment I just sat there, remembering the constant stream of nightmares I had been afflicted with as a child. They had faded when I hit adolescence to only an occasional nuisance, but this was the most vivid dream I had experienced in a while. Stress perhaps. I sighed, swung my feet off the end of the couch and onto the floor and studied the telephone morosely. I was expecting a call from an angel. That was a pretty stressful situation.

I was thirsty. I got up from the couch, took a moment to stretch some cramped muscles and padded across to my desk. I opened the top drawer, pushed my gun to one side and pulled out a can of soda that I had remembered I left there. I cracked the top and took a long draw from the can.

Something fell with a muffled bang. I jumped, turning sharply to look at the door that led through to the bathroom. There was a window above the cistern that led out into the alleyway. My heart began to pound again. Making as little noise as I could, I reached back into the drawer and pulled out my gun. I pulled back the hammer as gently as I could and held it up to eye-line, slowly moving towards the door.

The handle started to twist and I froze. I was only a few feet away by this point. The door was designed to open outward into the office and would swing out towards me. I took aim just above the handle.

The figure poked their head out from beyond the edge

of the door. I let them take one more step into the room before pushing the barrel of the gun against their temple and clearing my throat. "Can I help you?" I asked.

The figure froze, the cold steel of the revolver barrel pushing into the side of their head. Very slowly they began to raise their hands. "Please," the figure spoke calmly; it was a woman's voice. "Don't hurt me. I'm not here to kill you."

I blinked, withdrawing the weapon and stepping around to face her. I leaned over my desk and reached for the lamp on my table; I flicked it on and surveyed the intruder carefully.

She was in her early twenties and shorter than average, only a little over five feet. She had raven black hair and a tattoo down one cheek; esoteric symbols that looked like they had been picked up from a book on Ancient Egypt. She stood there, looking worried but unafraid. "I'm not here to kill you," she repeated calmly.

I frowned at her down the barrel of the gun. "You'll forgive me if I don't immediately believe you," I replied, "Given how you've just broken into my office and you feel the need to immediately reassure me about that specific situation."

The woman frowned a little. "I didn't know you'd be here," she replied. "I thought you'd be at home."

I pondered that thought; it was a reasonable assumption. If someone was trying to kill me, I imagine they would try to hit where I lived first; although for all I knew, there was another goon squad headed for my apartment as we spoke. So I kept my aim up at the woman and said, "Alright, so who are you and what are you doing here?"

The woman's eyes moved from the gun to me. "My name is Gemma," she said quietly. "I'm an Elioud, like you. I also know that you're working with an angel that calls himself Alleam."

Alarms started ringing in my head again and I tightened my grip on the revolver. "What the hell are you talking about?" I growled.

Gemma stared at me for a long moment with a quizzical expression. "You really don't know, do you?" she asked.

I took a step forward. "Lady, you better start making some sense soon or things are liable to get unpleasant," I warned, pointing the weapon straight at her face.

Gemma raised her hands even further in acknowledgement. "Okay, okay," she said hurriedly, her eyes back on the barrel of the gun. "I know you're working with Alleam because I represent a group of people that are tied to the paranormal world. We know that there's an angel working to stop the upcoming Apocalypse and he's been recruiting staff. Word on the grapevine is that you're gifted with powers of foresight and that he approached you to help him."

"Keep talking," I replied.

Gemma looked back up at my eyes. "We're a network of people like yourself; Eliouds who are embodied with powers by our ancestry. We're spread out across the country, listening and keeping an eye on the paranormal world for our own protection."

"That word again," I observed, frowning at her. "What's an Elioud?"

Gemma hesitated for a moment. "They...we," she corrected herself, "Are descendents of The Nephilim, who were the offspring of angels that lay with humans at the time of The First Fallen. That's where we get our powers from," she explained. "It comes down through the bloodline."

I observed her critically. "So you're saying you have powers too?" I asked sceptically. She nodded and I raised an eyebrow. "Alright then," I said. "Prove it to me."

Gemma gazed at me for a long moment. Then she flicked her wrist. The gun was torn from my hands by an invisible force and then flipped around to point at me. It hovered in mid-air for a moment and then went off with a loud roar, an unseen force squeezing the trigger. A moment later I was staring dumbstruck at a bullet less than five inches from my face. Gemma had one hand raised and turned palm-out towards the bullet. Then she repeated that flicking motion and the bullet flew gently to one side and dropped onto my desk with a rattle. Gemma looked back at me, her hands now hanging loosely by her hips. "Proof enough?" she asked with a slight quirk of her lips.

I swallowed and nodded. "Proof enough," I acknowledged, leaning back against my desk to get my thoughts straight. "That was incredible," I observed, glancing down at the bullet lying next to my hand.

Gemma tilted her head in thanks. "A lot of practice," she said. "We're all specialists in our particular powers; mine is telekinesis."

I nodded again. "So, what does this network of…Elioud do?" I asked, hesitating for a moment before using the unfamiliar word.

Gemma smiled a little; she seemed happy that I was being cooperative. "We protect each other," she said. "We're not particularly well-liked by angels due to our heritage, and the other side just tries to convert us into foot soldiers whenever they can." Gemma eyed me curiously. "That's why I was breaking in," she admitted. "We heard from some of our local contacts that Alleam had been in the area talking to you. That suggests that you're powerful at what you do. I wanted to see if I could find anything that suggested whether you'd be a threat to me and my own."

I smirked a little. "And what do you think so far?" I asked.

Gemma quirked an eyebrow. "Jury's still out," she responded. "But you didn't shoot me out of hand, so that says something."

I leaned back against my desk and folded my arms. "Alright," I said. "Let's presume for a moment that I believe you were just here checking out what side I am on. What other sides are there than Heaven and Alleam's gang?"

Gemma levelled me with an emotionless gaze. "Hell," she responded.

I raised both eyebrows, studying her face for any signs of humour. "Hell?" I repeated. "As in fire and brimstone and Satan?"

Gemma shrugged. "He prefers Lucifer," she corrected. "Satan is technically his title. But yes, that exact Hell is what I'm referring to."

I thought over my conversation with Jim earlier today. "The Los Hijos de la Parias," I muttered to myself quietly. "The Sons of the Pariah; they're the representatives of Hell?"

Gemma nodded. "That's right," she said. "It allows them to blend into human society in a way that still provides them with some privacy; biker gangs aren't exactly at the top of the list of whom most people want to spend time near."

I stood silently, contemplating the situation. "I need more information," I said, shaking my head.

Gemma grinned rather suddenly. "Well, you're in luck."

☦

The sky was still dark and the angelic compound was lit up like a football stadium. I was lying alongside Gemma at the summit of a hill behind the compound, keeping low in the undergrowth to avoid detection. My Lincoln had been stashed a few miles down the road, well out of sight of any potential bikers that may recognise it from the previous day's events. I could see the dozens of bikes parked outside the array of buildings. Reaching into a small rucksack I had brought, I pulled out a pair of binoculars. Risking as much exposure as I dared, I rose slightly and studied the people hurrying back and forth across the compound. "You're right," I said. "They're definitely in a rush to get things organised."

Gemma nodded, leaning in over my shoulder. I got a brief hint of a dark, floral perfume and had to mentally remind myself of the situation we were in. "There's a certain protocol that needs to be adhered to when the two sides meet," she observed. "It requires the full attendance of the senior-most terrestrial officials on both sides, with the leader of the visiting side being met by someone of at least equal rank from the hosting side."

I grunted. "Hence them clearing all the space for parking," I concluded, watching two Prospects hauling fuel barrels out of the centre of the courtyard. Then I frowned, training my binoculars towards the main gate on the far side of the compound. "What's that?" I muttered.

"What?" Gemma craned to see.

I pointed. Parked in front of the main compound gate was a large, black sedan that seemed very out of place next to the motorcycles. "Somebody important," I concluded quietly, watching the vehicle closely. A moment later, three men stepped out of a nearby building and paused by the sedan. One man was wearing a biker jacket and I recognised him from the recon photos as Banniel, the President of the angelic chapter. The other two wore dark suits and, by the way they glanced around, looked rather uncomfortable with their surroundings. I surmised from their dress sense and their roving eyes that they were some sort of security detail. One of the suited men turned and shook hands with Banniel before climbing into the car with his colleague, apparently about to leave. I took a mental note of the vehicle's registration plate whilst I had the chance. Then I watched Banniel gesture to another angel and the compound gates swung open. The black sedan disappeared from view as the gates swung closed again. I saw Banniel walk off to one side and lowered the binoculars. "What the hell was that about?" I wondered aloud.

"No idea," Gemma responded, craning her neck over the top of the ridge. "But we're running out of time, so we better get moving," she added, and went to stand.

I grabbed her shoulder. "What the hell do you think you're doing?" I hissed. I could see guards standing on the perimeter wall, submachine guns loose at their waists.

Gemma looked puzzled. "You wanted more information on what was going on, right?" she asked. Then she inclined her head down the hill, across a line of trees and foliage and towards a rear entrance gate. "We can use the terrain to hide ourselves down to the back door, and then we'll be able to sneak inside."

I stared at her. "You're crazy," I said incredulously.

She just tilted her head at me and frowned. "Hey, you wanted to see who you were dealing with," she retorted. She was scrambling down the hill towards the first tree line before I could even reply. I hesitated for a moment, unsure of whether to follow. She was right, I realised; I did want to know who I was dealing with. Besides, getting into the compound would help me understand the layout if I had to return. For all I knew, I could hear Banniel mention the identity of the Horseman tonight and be done with Alleam and his plans much sooner than I thought.

"Maybe I'm the crazy one," I muttered, shaking my head. Then I grabbed my rucksack, stuffed the binoculars back inside, and half-slid down the hill to catch up with Gemma.

We moved from tree to tree, keeping ourselves out of the line of sight of any of the guards on the perimeter wall. A moment's observation told us that they appeared to be changing position at brief intervals, thus giving us the possibility of being able to get inside without being spotted. By that point we had reached a small set of trees and bushes only fifty feet from the compound wall. We waited, holding our breath, until the nearest guard turned and began to move away. We dived towards the gate.

It was locked. "Damn it," I whispered in frustration. I glanced up at the wall, fearing at any moment that somebody would sound the alarm, or worse, simply open fire. "We need to get out of here," I whispered.

"Hang on," Gemma muttered. She was pressed against the door, feeling the material as if trying to seek something out. She closed her eyes and held one palm open a few inches from the lock, circling her hand slowly. I kept glancing upwards as the seconds dragged by, wondering how much longer our luck would hold out. I was just about to urge her again to leave when I heard the lock click and Gemma exhale. She pushed on the gate and it swung inwards with, thankfully, very little noise. She inclined her head around the door and, apparently seeing nothing, gestured for me to follow and disappeared through. Hesitating only for a split-second, I decided that I could not just leave her in there on her own and followed her through.

"This way," Gemma whispered, gesturing to me. I quietly pushed the gate closed behind us, hoping nobody would notice it was unlocked. We were in a small alleyway between one of the buildings and the compound wall. There were no guards in sight; I breathed a sigh of relief. Gemma was moving quietly down the alleyway towards another door; this one led into the rear of one of the buildings that looked out onto the compound. I followed her as closely as I could, keeping an eye out for anyone that may see us.

The door was unlocked and we slipped through. It was a garage, the opposite wall dominated by a large shutter door facing out onto the courtyard. A line of motorcycles stood in the gloom, lit only by small, high windows along either wall.

Nobody was inside. Gemma crept forward quietly towards the main door, turning and gesturing me to come closer. I edged around the line of bikes and crouched next to her, only a few feet from the shutter. "Now what?" I whispered as loudly as I dared. "We can't exactly see what's going on, can we?"

Gemma rolled her eyes at me. "You don't need to see, remember?" she hissed. "You just need to see," and she emphasised the last word to make her meaning clear.

I raised my eyebrows incredulously as I realised what she meant. "That's what this entire escapade was based on?" I whispered angrily. "I can't just make it happen whenever I want to."

Gemma frowned at me. "Of course you can, it's your gift," she retorted. "Just relax and focus."

I had to force myself to keep my voice down. "Yeah, because I've never thought about trying that before when I've wanted it to kick in," I snapped back, looking around the garage desperately. If we got caught in here, we were utterly screwed.

"Listen to me," Gemma hissed, and I felt her hand grab my chin and turn my head back towards her own. Her fingers were soft and warm and the gesture took me by surprise. "You can do this," she whispered gently, looking me directly in the eye. "Just close your eyes and imagine that you're looking through a window." She smiled encouragingly. "Trust me," she added.

I took a long, deep breath; we had come this far to get information; I might as well indulge her deluded belief in my abilities. So I turned towards the shutter door and closed my eyes, taking a few deep breaths and picturing a window forming in the grey steel of the door.

Nothing happened. I opened my eyes and exhaled in frustration. "This is ridiculous," I snapped at Gemma, shaking my head.

"Try again," Gemma replied. She cocked her head, her expression suddenly tense. "I can hear engines approaching, we don't have much time," she added.

I swore to myself and closed my eyes again. My heart was pounding and I forced myself to breathe deeply and slow my heart rate. "Window," I whispered to myself. "I am looking through a window, I am looking through-"

The dizziness overwhelmed me and I fell back onto the floor, barely missing one of the bikes. I felt Gemma grab me by the arm. "Are you okay?" she whispered, suddenly alarmed.

"Yeah," I replied breathlessly, trying to comprehend what I was seeing behind my tightly-screwed eyelids.

My visualisation of a window had suddenly become very real, as if I still had my eyes open. What I had not expected was to be mentally pulled through the window as if by some enormous vacuum effect. I could still feel the concrete of the garage floor underneath my legs, could smell the engine oil hanging in the air, but *I was standing in the centre of the courtyard*, a flurry of activity around me. I could see angels standing around, directing the human Prospects in clearing the courtyard. I could see the motorcycles parked in a row along one side, their chrome gleaming in the floodlights that surrounded me. I could see Banniel standing with a small group of angels, talking quietly and urgently to them. I could hear a cacophony of voices and engines and the wind in my ears and...

The dissonance it created alongside my true surroundings was starting to make me feel dizzy. I blocked out as much as I could and focused on observing what was happening. I saw Banniel turn and whistle, drawing the attention of everyone nearby. "Alright people, form up!" he shouted, his voice deep and laced with gravel. Everyone obeyed instantaneously, moving away from the entrance gate and assembling themselves in disciplined lines. Banniel took his place front and centre.

"What can you see?" Gemma whispered in one ear.

"They're organising the reception party," I muttered, trying to ignore the constant feeling of nausea in my gut. "Looks like they're about ready to – yeah, here we go," I added.

"Open the gate," Banniel shouted, and I saw him gesture to one of the angels standing by the front entrance. The angel turned and pushed a switch mounted to the wall and the gates began to grind open. I could hear the rumble of engines and headlight beams in the rapidly-growing entrance way.

And then Hell rolled in.

Chapter 7

"Oh hell," I muttered, and I meant it literally. The convoy of bikes roared into the angelic compound in two disciplined lines, their bikes made of black metal and blood red fixtures, the symbol on their jackets depicting a pair of crossed, flaming torches adorned with their club name. They circled the opposite side of the compound once, turning so that they fanned out with their bikes facing the angels on the opposite side. Then they came to a halt in rank formation, a single rider sat at the head of their procession. On some invisible cue, each biker twisted back on their throttles and let a mighty roar of engines out into the sky. The sound was ferocious and I involuntarily went to cover my ears. The angels stood unmoved by this ferocious display; Banniel's expression did not change even slightly from the cool, neutral gaze he had fixed upon the lead Hell rider. After almost ten seconds of that immense, intimidating cacophony, they turned off their engines and the whole world went silent.

The lead rider unseated from his bike and removed his mirrored helmet. The face behind it was cruel and sneering; a pair of blood red eyes underneath a shock of hair the same colour. Several scars adorned his cheeks, all faded with age apart from a newly-inflicted one that still held stitches along its length. He surveyed the angels contemptuously, his helmet held loosely under one arm. After a long moment, he stepped forward into the empty space between both assembled groups. I watched Banniel do the same. Summoning up all the courage I had, I stepped forward mentally until I stood next to them. Fear and nausea aside, I had to hear this.

I watched Banniel observe the other man quietly for a moment, a complete lack of emotion on his face. Then he bowed his head in a stiff, formal gesture and said, "Astartoth,

I bid thee welcome." He paused for a moment before adding, "Custom normally dictates that the Presidents attend to such matters themselves. Where is Beelzebub?"

Astartoth grinned, a gesture that I found remarkably unpleasant. "The President is currently involved in other matters that require his attention," he replied, a slight sneer in his tone. "Custom only dictates that visiting delegates are met by an equal or superior rank of the host. As Vice-President of the Satan Lucifer's delegation here on this temporal plane, I am fully authorised by Beelzebub to attend to this matter myself."

Banniel's face twitched with what I thought may have been annoyance, but it disappeared as quickly as it had arrived. "Very well," he said quietly, and drew himself to his full height. "The duly appointed delegation of The Holy Throne tasked with His Will upon Earth in this matter of Apocalypse wishes to complain in the strongest possible terms to the delegation of Satan for breaches of Treaty." Banniel's voice was now louder and more commanding, clearly projected for the benefit of everyone assembled. He levelled his eyes at Astartoth. "Such Treaty violations may result in the severest of penalties," the angel added, an undertone of threat in his otherwise calm voice.

Astartoth grinned again, and I realised why the gesture made me so uncomfortable; he had far too many teeth. "And what breaches may the delegation of the Throne be referring to?" he asked with mocking politeness.

Banniel's face did not change. "Yesterday, two members of the fallen were engaged in some kind of overt action just beyond the very walls of this compound," he stated matter-of-factly. "Thus putting the Satanic delegation in breach of at least two Articles of Treaty, concerning overt Satanic combat activity on Earth before the agreed time, and the neutrality of designated temporal embassies."

Astartoth laughed aloud. It was an unpleasant cackle, like a murder of crows all crying out at once, and it echoed around the walls of the compound as if seeking escape. "You brought me here to answer such flimsy accusations?" he said, snorting with derisive humour at his angelic counterpart. "We breached no neutrality of embassy; the alleged events took place beyond these walls. Your attempts to criminalise our rights to oversee your work are pathetic." Astartoth smiled at Banniel. "As for the first charge," he continued. "Those actions were the work of rogue agents of the Satan's Host trying to neutralise something they perceived to be a threat to our security. They have been dealt with internally."

I saw Banniel's face twitch again, the glimmer of a smirk as his eyes flicked to the newly healing scar on Astartoth's face. "So I can see," he remarked. I saw Astartoth's face flicker with anger. Banniel continued, "The Holy Throne would like to stress to the Satanic delegation that this is the fourth instance of 'rogue agent' activity that has occurred in the last month." Banniel emphasised the words 'rogue agent' to express his disbelief. "We would like to officially notify the representatives of Satan that any more instances of him being unable to control his armies will result in an abrogation of Treaty and all the penalties that would entail."

Astartoth's face twisted with anger, but I could see him visibly restrain himself; there must be some pretty strong agreements on neutrality in these meetings, I realised. "So noted," Astartoth spat back. Then he grinned unsettlingly again. "However, there is one further point that I would like to raise concerning the matter; one of grave potential consequences."

I saw Banniel raise an eyebrow. "Oh?" he said, suddenly wary.

Astartoth nodded, his face split with that unsettling number of teeth. "Yes indeed," he confirmed. "Interrogation of our rogue operatives has led us to some disturbing information about some of your Heavenly associates." He used the word 'Heavenly' with a distinct sneer in his voice. "Those operatives have sworn to us that they came under attack by a servant of the Holy Throne." Astartoth then raised his voice for all to hear. "Furthermore, they declare that this action was witnessed by a member of your very own delegation."

I swore to myself, scanning the crowd as Banniel eyed Astartoth carefully. Then I saw her standing at the back of the crowd, trying to look as inconspicuous as possible. I turned and saw Astartoth staring directly at her and my heart skipped a beat. "Who is this accusation levelled at?" I heard Banniel ask stiffly.

Astartoth stared at her for a long moment, wicked grin still plastered across his face. "One of your human helpers," he responded, and pointed directly at her. "The Sister Miriam, to be precise."

The air suddenly went tense. I saw Miriam look up with astonishment. "What?" she asked, looking around in alarm.

Banniel turned to look at her directly. "What is your specific accusation?" he asked Astartoth in a stern tone, his eyes still fixed on Miriam.

Astartoth folded his arms triumphantly. "Our rogue agents were in the process of trying to destroy an Elioud they believed was a threat to our security; an unsanctioned action, of course," he added, smiling mockingly at the front row of the angelic bikers. "Our agents declared that they saw the Sister Miriam in direct contact with this Elioud." He turned to look at Banniel. "Did she report this?" he asked sweetly, already knowing the answer from the angelic President's body language.

Banniel continued to stare at Miriam. "She did not," he replied.

Miriam looked pleadingly at Banniel. "My Lord, I…"

she began.

Banniel held up his hand and she fell silent. "A matter for which she will be dealt with internally," he added, finally turning back to Astartoth. "Just as your own…rogue agents were," he added with a faint trace of a smile.

Astartoth shook his head. "Not good enough," he declared loudly. "Under Treaty agreements, we came here to answer your charges on rogue activities by members of the Satan's Host. It was reported through the proper channels as a threat to security and has been answered." He gazed at Miriam. "The nun did not report her part in this matter, thus leaving her suspect to involvement with this Elioud and abrogating her protection under Treaty for being part of a threat to the Satanic delegate's security." Astartoth cocked his head slightly and licked his lips, like a predator that had identified its next meal. "We demand she be handed over for punishment," he declared.

"Not going to happen," Banniel replied without hesitation. The atmosphere suddenly went very tense.

From somewhere just beyond my senses, I felt Gemma nudge me. "What's going on?" she whispered urgently.

"They're trying to compromise my contact on the inside," I whispered, trying to think of something. If Astartoth got his way, there went my internal source of information and my key way of getting close to Banniel. I saw Astartoth's expression turn ugly. He took a step forward and I saw everyone on both sides of the meeting suddenly shift their weight slightly in preparation. "That's a violation of Treaty," he said to Banniel in a low, dangerous tone.

"It's a technicality," Banniel shot back. "Something, I might add, that your side has wiggled out of on multiple occasions by citing the spirit and not the letter of the agreement." Banniel drew himself to his full height. "The Sister Miriam will be dealt with internally," he declared. "We have no evidence of this perceived threat to the Satan's Host by this alleged Elioud you claim your 'rogue' agents were after."

"We *will* take her," Astartoth whispered furiously, his blood red eyes beginning to glow with intensity.

Banniel smirked and clenched his fists, stepping even closer to his Satanic counterpart. "Just try it," he said slowly.

"Damn it," I muttered to myself. "They're about to go to war over this. We've got to do something."

I heard Gemma swear to herself. "Okay, but you're going to hate me for this," I heard her say. Then I heard her stand up.

"What're you-?" I began, and then had to stop myself from shouting aloud. Without warning, I saw several of the fuel barrels in one corner of the courtyard leap into the air with barely a sound. With all the tension between both sides, nobody noticed them arcing into the air until they were on their way back down. Somebody cried out. I saw both Banniel and Astartoth snap their heads in the direction of the threat. The barrels came crashing down with a massive crash, bursting at the seams and sending gallons of fuel across the compound floor.

I opened my eyes, my vision rushing back into my body as if I had been catapulted on a giant piece of elastic. I fell backwards onto the floor and shook my head. The garage walls were around me once again, the gloom a stark contrast to the floodlights that had been in the courtyard. I turned and glared open-mouthed at Gemma, who was now stood up and, eyes closed, was motioning with her hands as if conducting an orchestra. I heard more crashes from beyond the garage doors as yet further mayhem came crashing down around the angels. Cries of alarm and activity outside indicated that they were recovering from the initial surprise. "What the hell are you doing?" I hissed.

"Saving your friend's life," Gemma said, her eyes still

closed. She gestured both hands outwards forcefully. I heard the muffled sound of steel being torn outside. "Gate's open," she then said, opening her eyes and blinking a few times. "That should give us enough time to get out of here," she surmised.

"And how exactly do we do that now that everyone is on full alert?" I hissed. And then I saw that Gemma was staring at one of the motorcycles. "Oh hell," I muttered.

"If you have any other ideas, I'd like to hear them," Gemma said. She was already climbing onto the bike, grabbing the helmet slung on the handlebars and pulling it onto her head.

"I haven't been on anything with less than four wheels for years," I hissed, my mind whirling. I could hear raised voices out in the courtyard. The situation was getting more dangerous with every passing moment.

Gemma reached across to the next motorcycle in the row and scooped the helmet from its handlebars, throwing it to me. "Now's the time for a refresher course," she replied.

I froze for a moment, trying to think of any other way out of the situation. The voices were getting louder and angrier beyond the courtyard, so I swore under my breath and climbed onto the bike. The keys were already in the ignition and I reached down to it. "If we die, I'll kill you," I shouted over my shoulder as I twisted the key and felt the bike shudder to life.

With one swift motion of her hands, Gemma blew the shutter door off its hinges and sent it flying across the courtyard. Light flooded in, piercing the gloom of the garage that had been our sanctuary up until this point. The scene was utter chaos; human helpers attempting to clear up fuel barrels that had been thrown everywhere whilst angels and their fallen counterparts were squaring up to each-other as if about to start a massive brawl, both sides thinking that the other had caused the trick with the barrels. That all came to a halt when the garage door went flying across the concrete and everyone shifted their attention to us. I checked the clasp on the helmet and leant forward over the handlebars. "Hold on!" I shouted, and twisted the throttle.

The Harley leapt forward with a roar, aiming right for the front gate that Gemma had earlier thrown from its hinges. She tightened her arms around my waist as we rocketed forward in a cloud of exhaust and burning rubber. People went diving in all directions; I caught a fleeting glance of Astartoth's enraged expression as we blew past him and out of the front gate. I kicked up a gear and switched on the bike's headlights, aiming for the road beyond the compound's driveway.

"Watch out!" Gemma shouted, and a second later I heard a terrific roar of noise blow past my ear. They were shooting at us – no, I realised as I heard another roar and saw a ball of blue energy explode into a tree just to our left. They were using some kind of angelic magic on us. I began swerving as rapidly as I dared to throw off their aim, diving in between several trees and out onto the tarmac. I leant steeply to my left and swept the bike around towards Chicago, twisting the throttle handle back to the stopper. For a few moments we were alone, the dark road lit by the bike's single headlight, the wind blasting past us at increasing speed. I was just contemplating slowing down when I heard Gemma call out again. "They're following us!" she cried.

"What?" I shouted, and dared a glance back over my shoulder. Sure enough, a long convoy of headlights were approaching us from behind at a rapid pace. "Oh, you've got to be kidding me," I muttered to myself, turning back to the road and scanning frantically for some way to escape. Then I saw an On-Ramp sign for Interstate 57 and grimaced. "Hang on!" I shouted again, and twisted the bike into a sharp turn to the left. The bike tore up the incline, nearly side-swiping a truck as we joined the main road and I pulled the throttle back to the stopper. I had been hoping for some traffic to help me lose the bikers, but aside from the truck now shrinking in my rear view mirrors the road was almost deserted at this early time in the morning. There was no other choice now; we had to keep going. I leant forward and kept increasing speed, pushing the Harley to its limit and darting around the few other vehicles on the road as nimbly as I could.

"They're still gaining on us!" Gemma shouted.

I glanced over my shoulder and, sure enough, they were. I swore to myself and turned back to the road. "We can't lose them like this!" I shouted back to her, glancing down at my speedometer. The Harley was at its limit, the engine whining at the top of its capacity, and yet the angels were still gaining on us.

"Then we'll just have to get inventive!" Gemma shouted. I felt her twist in her seat and reach her arms out towards the angels. As we rocketed past a row of construction equipment parked by the side of the road, she swept her hands up in a graceful, orchestral motion and threw both hands out again. I watched in one of the bike's side mirrors as an entire earth-mover lifted into the air and went flying back down the road. I saw the angel's headlights scatter as the giant machine hit the road and started rolling, breaking apart with a rending of metal and smashing glass. A few of the bikes got through, nimbly avoiding the debris across the road and continued after us. Gemma focused her attention directly on the bikes, sweeping her hands around then throwing her weight so violently to one side that I almost lost control of the bike. I watched in the mirrors as the surviving bikers suddenly had their handlebars torn from their grip and thrown full-lock to the left. The bikes went over with a crash I heard over the engine, and their riders went tumbling along the road at literal breakneck speeds.

I heard Gemma let out a whoop of victory and shout a few unkind words back in the direction of the bikers. "That should get them off our backs" She shouted at me with a tone of elation. I said nothing, concentrating on the road ahead, my heart pounding in my ears.

☦

We dumped the bike on the outskirts of Southern Chicago, leaving it in an abandoned lot where nobody would be able to easily spot it. We had rode the rest of the journey back without any further problem from the angels; it seemed that wipe-out on the Interstate had discouraged them from following us at this time. Nonetheless, I doubted that was the last I would be hearing of them. We walked a couple of blocks and then hailed a cab. I directed the driver to a cheap motel that I knew; I was pretty sure that the angels would have got a good look at who I was this time and was reluctant to go back to either my office or my apartment. We rode in the cab in silence; I was angry, and I got the impression that Gemma could sense it. She offered no statements until we were out of the cab and into one of the motel rooms when she turned to me, spread her arms and said, "So what's your problem? We're alive, aren't we?"

I closed the door and turned to her with a furious expression my face. "Yeah, we're alive!" I spat. "And for what? You drag me into the lion's den, you put my main contact in jeopardy and then you put me in danger by letting them see my face in that ridiculous escape plan of yours!"

Gemma folded her arms defensively. "They may have seen what you look like, but they didn't kill you," she said sharply. "I made sure of that on the Interstate – you're welcome, by the way," she added sarcastically.

"Oh yeah, sure; thanks for that," I replied, mirroring

Gemma's sarcasm in such a way that it made her blink in surprise. "And setting aside the massive amount of wreckage you've now left across the Interstate, how do you know the bikers that you took out weren't humans?" I glared at her pointedly.

Gemma opened her mouth to say something, but then closed it. "I…" she said a moment later, before shrugging. "I didn't think of that," she acknowledged. Then she looked up at me again. "But they were out to hurt us, and I saved us from that," she retorted. "It's them or us, and that's quite simply the facts." Then she smiled slightly. "Besides, if we hadn't been there, we couldn't have saved your friend from potentially being captured and tortured by Astartoth," she added. "It's not like you were willing to do anything with your abilities to help her."

I looked up sharply and saw her staring me straight in the eye. "Get out," I said quietly.

Gemma cocked her head at me and shook it slightly. "You know, I've been where you have," she said gently. "Most Elioud have had to deal with it when they were young. The persecution, the bullying; we all get exposed to it the moment we let someone else see our abilities." Gemma took a step forward, her tone becoming more earnest. "But you have to see, we can do so much good; we can protect so many people."

"Get out!" I shouted, and glared at her. "I didn't ask for these abilities," I hissed through clenched teeth. "I didn't ask to be different from everyone else, and I certainly didn't ask to be dragged into a literal battle between Heaven and Hell." I bowed my head, suddenly very exhausted. "Just leave me alone," I muttered.

Gemma stood silently for a moment. "Fine," she said, and I heard her open the door. "At some point, you're going to have to accept your gift, Sam," she said quietly. "It will save your life one day." She began to step out of the door and paused again. "Alleam," she said a moment later. "He didn't tell you about the bikers from Hell being on Earth. There's a lot else he hasn't told you." She sighed and stepped out into the cool night air. "You should be careful about trusting him," she added quietly, and closed the door. And with that, I was alone again.

Chapter 8

The telephone startled me out of my sleep.

At first I was confused, staring around the unfamiliar room through the bleary eyes of someone who had missed a lot of sleep recently. Then I remembered checking into the Motel the night before due to my security worries. I sat up in the bed and kicked my feet over the side, rubbing my head with a mournful groan as I listened to the telephone ring for me.

The telephone was ringing for me.

I looked up sharply, staring at the device as it continued to ring. I had told nobody I was staying here; I had not even enquired about what telephone number directed people to my room. I glanced towards the window and then back to the telephone. Perhaps I had been followed after all; Gemma's assurances had hardly made me feel particularly safe last night. I reached across to the bedside table and picked up the receiver. Holding it to my ear hesitantly, I said, "Hello?"

"The Sister Miriam is safe," a voice responded. It was that strange, androgynous voice from a few days before, the one that had directed me to the angel's compound on behalf of Alleam. "She will be in the city on errands at 11am today. You will meet her at the following address." At that, the voice rattled out an intersection in downtown Chicago, not much of a distance from the Motel.

"I'll be there," I replied, before adding, "How did you get this number?"

The voice exhaled; if I was a gambling man, I would have bet it was some kind of amused snort. "How did you think I could not?" it asked ominously, and then the line buzzed clear. I looked at the receiver for a long moment, glanced back at the window, and then began to redial. I would have time for one quick meeting beforehand.

☩

I pulled the black, dilapidated sedan up onto the corner of the downtown intersection. My Lincoln was still hidden an hour south of the city where Gemma and I had left it the previous evening; I made a mental note to call a tow company and get it hauled back when I had a moment. There was a rental company just down the road from the motel, so a swift transaction later and I had wheels to get to my meeting with Jim.

    The police officer was leaning against his cruiser with a raised eyebrow as he saw me pull up. His face cracked into a broad smile as I parked up behind him and got out of the car. "Finally got rid of that death-trap, I see?" he teased in the manner that a long-time friend can do. Then his smile faded as I came closer. "Jesus man, you look awful."

    I flinched a little at the religious expletive, a little weary of so much holiness as of late, and nodded with a tired smile. "It's been a rough couple of nights," I said. Then I saw Jim's face take on that professionally enquiring look and I hastily added, "All-night surveillance."

    "Uh-huh," Jim replied, not looking particularly convinced. "So what did you need to talk to me about that couldn't wait until I was off patrol?"

    I reached into my pocket and pulled out a piece of paper. I had scribbled down a few things before I went to sleep, desperate to keep them in mind. "This vehicle registration," I said, handing it over. "Very out of place at the location I was surveying."

    Jim took the paper, looking dubious. "You know I can't tell you any personal information," he said, looking back up at me.

I nodded. "I know; just anything to do with affiliations to the Angeles de la Muerte would be useful."

Jim sighed, looking back at the piece of paper. "Wait here," he said, and climbed back into his cruiser.

I leaned against the rear bumper as Jim typed away at the police database, jumping at anything that sounded like a motorcycle engine. I needed some good sleep soon, I realised. Jim climbed back out a few moments later with an odd look on his face. I turned and eyed him as he walked back towards me, already sensing something unpleasant in the information he had. "Anything you can tell me?" I asked.

Jim handed me back the piece of paper. "It's a government vehicle," he said. "It's listed as a Secret Service armoured car, to be precise."

I raised my eyebrows, completely taken aback. "What the hell is a car used by the Secret Service doing in a biker compound in the middle of the night?" I wondered aloud.

Jim pursed his lips. "I don't know," he said. "But with the President and the Vice-President flying in shortly, I'm going to have to push this up the chain and see what I can find out." I opened my mouth to respond, to tell Jim to leave it alone, but he held up a hand firmly. "I've got to check this out, Sam," he said in a business-like tone. "We're talking about potential security threats to the President here. No arguments."

I sighed. "Fine," I said. "Just keep my name out of it if you can." Jim nodded. I glanced at my watch and back up to him. "I've got to go," I said. "I have a contact to meet."

Jim nodded, turning back to his car. "Be careful out there," he said over his shoulder, before climbing into the car and starting the engine. I watched the police cruiser roll away into traffic and I leaned back against the hood of my own car, deep in thought. Secret Service personnel visiting angels; perhaps they had contacts in the government. I sighed and rubbed my temples, a wave of tiredness flowing over me. This was getting stranger by the moment.

"Ahem."

I looked up and saw Miriam standing on the sidewalk a few paces from me, glancing nervously in either direction. She was wearing a non-descript black tee and blue jeans similar to what I had seen her wear when we first met. Her biker jacket hung tightly from one gripped hand, evidently removed so as not to draw attention. I straightened up quickly and tilted my head towards the car. Miriam nodded and followed me to the vehicle, climbing into the passenger seat. When the doors were closed, I turned to her. "Are you okay?" I asked with genuine concern.

She nodded, fretting at her lower lip. Her eyes kept roving the sidewalk as if expecting something to jump out at any moment. After the past couple of days, I did not fault her. "Yeah," she said softly, before rubbing her eyes with a sigh. I got the impression she had slept little as well. "After you pulled your escape act, the Hell delegation left for security reasons," she continued. "I managed to convince Banniel that I had simply stopped to help you fix your car and that I knew nothing else about you."

I frowned. "They can't do some kind of magical lie detector or anything?" I asked, genuinely interested.

Miriam glanced up sharply, perhaps reading my tone as initially mocking or suspicious. When she saw the genuine curiosity on my face she relaxed a little and shook her head. "Doesn't work like that," she said wearily. "Seers are pretty rare in the angelic hierarchy nowadays, and most of the ones they have are nowhere near as powerful as they used to be." Her mouth twitched and her eyes momentarily took on a distant gaze. "Alleam had me trained and protected to deal with those sorts of situations," she added after a moment, as if recalling an unpleasant memory.

I decided not to press further. Instead I asked, "How do

I get to Banniel?"

Miriam pondered for a moment. "He's closely guarded at all times," she said eventually. "He does not leave the compound very often either; only for highly important meetings elsewhere."

I nodded, making mental notes. "Any such meetings coming up?" I asked.

Miriam shook her head slowly. "Nothing outside of the compound," she said. Then she paused and fretted her lip again, seemingly very reluctant to talk. "I know there's a VIP meeting coming up," she said. "They were discussing the security requirements this morning. I'm part of a group tasked with making arrangements for the compound to be appropriately sanctified and secured."

I frowned. "Sanctified?" I asked.

Miriam nodded. "A ritual with effects on angels and similar creatures," she said. "It's a security system of sorts; when the compound has been ritually sanctified, only appropriately blessed individuals are able to enter the compound without setting off the paranormal radar of every angel present." She glanced out of the window, avoiding looking at me at all costs. "It prevents human outsiders and members of Hell's forces on Earth getting into important, private meetings."

"Why is this sanctification not always in place?" I asked.

"It normally is," Miriam replied. "But it was disengaged as a courtesy to the representatives of Hell during last night's meeting." The outline of a smile traced briefly across her lips. "It makes them feel...rather unpleasant," she added. "But now they have left, the sanctification can be put back into place."

I nodded, thoughts whirring through my head. "It must be an important meeting," I said. "Perhaps even involving the Horseman."

Miriam bit her lip at the remark, continuing to stare out

of the window. "It's the only major representative of Heaven on Earth that I can think would need this much security," she said, her tone carefully neutral.

I glanced sidelong at her. "You don't like talking about this, do you?" I asked.

Miriam turned to look directly at me; that took me by surprise. She smirked without humour. "I'm a traitor," she said, bitterness evident in her voice. "I am helping out my Lord Alleam because I know he is right. But I am still a traitor." She sighed again. "I am violating every vow I made when I took up the Holy Orders," she reflected. "I was directly chosen by the Lord Banniel to be part of the Heavenly Ministry on Earth, to take part in this most holy of tasks. I believe the world will find salvation in the arms of our Lord God and those who have sinned should be punished." Miriam quickly turned to look back out of the window. She hesitated for a long time. "But I have a sister," she said eventually. "I have a sister who is a sinner and continues to sin, and yet she is a good person at heart. She yet may find redemption, and I cannot let her be damned before she does."

I looked at Miriam for a long moment, unable to think of anything to say that would ease her self-torment. So instead I gently asked, "When is the meeting?"

Miriam sniffed. "I don't know yet," she said. "I've been instructed to pick up some of the supplies we need today. Once I know, I will contact you through the usual telephone number and we'll have to quickly arrange you being sanctified for entry into the compound." She glanced once more at me. "I have to go," she said. "They'll be expecting me back soon." She reached for the door handle.

I leant over gently and put one hand on her shoulder. She flinched a little and I retracted my arm a few inches to show I meant no harm. "Thank-you," I said quietly. "I know how hard this must be for you."

She snorted, shaking her head. "No you don't," she replied, and climbed out of the car. She pushed the door closed behind her and, with a quick glance both ways along the sidewalk, started walking quickly away.

I watched her as she left, deep in thought. In truth, I felt sorry for her; she was obviously struggling with the turmoil between her faith and concern for her sister. She was a scared young person working against the very faith she had sworn to uphold, surrounded by beings of unimaginable power that were plotting the downfall of the entire world. Frankly, I was impressed she was holding it together as well as she was. I sighed, started the engine and pulled the rental out into traffic, intending to head back to my office.

"You should not get too close," Alleam said.

I shouted aloud in surprise, losing control of the wheel and almost swerving into the oncoming lane. An oncoming sedan had to brake sharply and honked their horn angrily at me as I drove past. I reasserted control and looked across at the passenger seat. Alleam was sat there, calmly gazing out of the front window, wearing the same charcoal grey suit that I had seen him in a few days before. "For the love of-" I began and then stopped before getting to the expletive, presuming that taking the Lord's name in vain in front of a literal angel was probably not the best thing to do. So instead I just glared at him and exclaimed, "Can you not do that?"

Alleam turned to look at me, a vague sense of puzzlement on his face. "I'm sorry?" he asked.

"The sudden appearances," I emphasised, gesturing at him with an upturned palm. "Unless you want me to be joining your former compatriots up amongst the clouds before I get this job done for you."

Alleam's mouth twitched slightly. "What makes you think you would be going up?" he asked quietly.

I glanced at him again, trying to work out if he was being humorous. He just stared at me, so instead I looked back at the road and asked, "What do you want?"

Alleam turned to gaze back out of the windshield. "I need you to do a task for me," he said.

I laughed. Alleam looked over at me again, this time in vague surprise. "You're kidding, right?" I said incredulously, gripping the steering wheel tightly with a building anger. "You've already got me trying to conduct espionage against a person of such power and authority that I cannot possibly start to comprehend whilst dealing with his entourage of angelic heavy-hitters and - oh yeah," and here I snapped my fingers in a mocking manner as if pretending to remember something. "You neglected to mention that the literal spawn of Hell is also up here too and is trying to kill me." I fell into silence, taking several deep breaths to try and calm both my heart rate and the likely-suicidal desire to take a swing at Alleam.

I felt Alleam's eyes on me for a long minute. "Yes," he said. "The Sister Miriam told me about your little stunt at the compound last night. How did you manage to get in?"

I hesitated for a moment, casting my mind back to Gemma's comments on Heaven and their stance on her and the circle of Elioud that surrounded her. I wondered why Miriam had not mentioned that I had someone with me when I blew out of there on the bike, although it had all happened so fast she may not have noticed. "Their human security got lax and I got lucky," I finally said. "I wanted to try my luck at getting some information from Banniel and getting this whole damned affair over with as soon as possible. I ended up right in the middle of a meeting between both sides." I looked back over at Alleam. "Why didn't you tell me about them?" I asked in a calmer tone.

Alleam sighed; I was a little surprised, as I had not heard him do that so far. It seemed weary, as if this question had come up before. "Contact with Hell's forces is highly corrupting," he answered. "Your role in all of this has not required you to be exposed to them up until now." He then rubbed his forehead with his palm, a remarkably human gesture that I found unexpected. "I was trying to protect you from coming into contact with them," he added.

I smiled slightly. "Well, apparently they were gunning for me right from the start," I said, recalling the attack outside the compound a few days earlier and my rescue by Anahita. Then I frowned. "Why are they gunning for me?" I asked, glancing at Alleam.

Alleam did not answer for a long moment. "I do not know," he finally replied. "Perhaps they want to turn you to their side, perhaps they have some vested interest in the Apocalypse occurring." He glanced at me again. "My primary concern is making sure we get the Horseman, not the machinations of our eternally damned cousins."

I acknowledged his comments with a tilt of the head, recognising the size of the task ahead. "I'm a little unclear on why Hell gets to send people up here during the Apocalypse," I remarked. "They were being pretty diplomatic last night for two groups that are supposed to be waging a literal war for the human soul; kept mentioning treaty obligations of some sort."

Alleam was quiet for a moment; I glanced at him and saw a faint trace of conflict in his eyes, as if he was debating whether to elaborate on my musings. He must have then decided, because he leaned back in the seat and looked over at me. "It is to do with what your species sees as the Book of Revelation," he answered. "The Book is actually derived from a treaty signed between Almighty God and the Satan Lucifer that deals with the End Times." Alleam looked back out of the windshield. "It is too complicated to go into the details of right now," he continued. "Suffice to say, part of the treaty stipulates that Hell has a right to send observers to oversee Heaven's management of the Apocalypse, in order to make sure that it is being carried out as per the original procedure agreed in the Treaty of Revelation."

I nodded to myself, processing this information. "There was a United States government vehicle at the compound just before I broke in," I said, almost slipping and saying 'we' instead. "It was a vehicle owned by those who protect our President. Any idea why they would be involved?"

Alleam shook his head. "I know little about earthly governmental affairs," he replied. "Both sides do have contacts at various levels of government across the world. I will investigate using my own sources and see how this may connect."

I nodded again. "Why do you guys need to use humans in all of this?" I asked curiously. "I mean, you're angels; you're the instruments of God's will. Aren't you supposed to be all-powerful?"

Alleam glanced at me as if I had touched a nerve. "There are limits to our powers on Earth," he said simply. "We derive our power from the faith of those who believe in us." Alleam leaned in to the passenger window and looked up towards the sky briefly; I swore I saw a look of longing in his eyes. "There's a lot less belief about than in times past," he said softly. "That's part of the reason why all this is happening." Then he straightened in his seat and looked back towards me, as if suddenly self-conscious. "Also," he conceded, "Angels and their fallen counterparts are not as proficient at interaction with humans, although the fallen find it easier due to their greater contact with the human population during their attempts to corrupt. Many of us do not have much experience with the day-to-day economic and social aspects of living in your societies. Having faithful servants amongst the human population solves those issues."

I was silent for a few moments. "You still haven't told

me why you're here," I noted. "Some kind of task, you said?"

Alleam nodded. "I need you to make contact with somebody," he said. "Turn right here."

We drove in silence for a long time, making our way across the traffic of the city and out into more residential areas. Alleam eventually directed me to pull up outside a rundown, seedy looking bar just off the intersection. We were in Auburn Gresham, one of the most dangerous areas of Chicago. Dishevelled, two-storey red bricks lined either side of the road. There were very few people on the streets, and that made me even more nervous. "Lovely neighbourhood your friend chooses to live in," I remarked, glancing in my rear view mirror to check behind us.

"He's not a friend," Alleam replied shortly, and I glanced over at him as I noted his tone. Alleam was staring at the bar. "I need you to go in there and ask for a man named Furcas," he said, nodding to the bar's front door.

I glanced over at the bar, its darkened, dirt-smeared windows allowing little visibility inside. I looked back at Alleam. "And who exactly is that?" I asked.

Alleam glanced at me with a look of irritation similar to that I had seen in my office when we first met. "He's the Sergeant-At-Arms for the Los Hijos de la Parias and the third-ranking member of the Hell delegation," he explained. "And we need him for information."

I raised my eyebrows incredulously. "Are you fucking high?" I exclaimed, looking back at the bar. "These are the people that are specifically trying to track me down and kill me; you want me to walk in there and literally ask one of them outside for a chat?"

Alleam glared at me. "Our best information tells us that Furcas has not yet been let into the loop about who you are," He said irritably. "I am not able to enter and your extremely strong powers of precognition make you the only one that stands a chance of getting out of there alive."

"And why exactly can you not go in yourself?" I asked in a disbelieving tone. "I would have thought that another angel would have better chance than me."

Alleam sighed audibly. "Miriam told you about the sanctification rituals, yes?" he asked. I nodded and Alleam continued. "Well, there are different levels of it. At the highest level, nobody unsanctified, either human or angel can enter that area. According to the Treaty of Revelation, this level is reserved for the delegation compounds only." Alleam nodded at the bar. "However, there is a lower level of sanctification that just prevents angels from entering and not humans," he explained. "We've known this place to be a secret outpost of Hell for a while now; they use it as a sanctuary to hide weapons and residents of Hell that are not officially allowed up here according to our agreements."

I frowned. "And Heaven lets them get away with that?" I asked.

Alleam shrugged. "No different from how your terrestrial governments hide secret bases in other countries," he said. "Heaven knows about them, but the resulting potential confrontation by bringing up their existence makes it worthwhile to keep quiet." Alleam smirked a little. "Besides, Heaven has several of its own as well."

I sighed, looking back at the bar. "This is insane," I muttered, and then louder I said, "Alright, what do I do?"

Alleam nodded to himself, apparently pleased by my agreement. "Walk in there and ask for Furcas," he said. "Tell him that Asmodeus has a message for him. That should get him outside quite easily and I can handle the rest."

I glanced at Alleam, quirking an eyebrow. "Sure, piece of cake," I muttered. Then I shook my head briefly in astonishment at what I had got myself into, climbed out of the car and walked across to the bar.

Inside the entrance it was dark and cool. I blinked a few times to let my eyes adjust to the light. The bar was as dank and uninviting as it had looked outside. A row of decrepit red-leather booths stretched away along one wall opposite the bar. Several ceiling fans whirled uselessly, doing nothing to help the heat of the day. An old jukebox in the corner was blaring out some old rock and roll.

There were three people in the bar; the barman, who looked up sharply as the door closed behind me, and two bikers sitting at the bar and nursing bottles of beer. Their leather jackets showed they were members of the Los Hijos. They took seemingly no notice of my entrance. I felt remarkably over-dressed in the shirt and jeans I was wearing.

I walked over to the bar slowly, the barman never taking his eyes off me. I leaned against the bar and nodded politely. The barman did not move, continuing to stare at me. I swallowed nervously. "I'm looking for Furcas," I said.

The bartender stiffened slightly, but continued not to say a word. I noticed that he had a set of numbers printed on the back of one of his hands. It was one of the bikers who spoke. He did not look up from his beer, but he raised his head by a barely perceptible degree and said gruffly, "Who wants him?"

I cleared my throat, taking a quick glance around the bar for the nearest exit. A sign across the room pointed down a brief corridor for the toilets, and from where I stood I could vaguely perceive a fire door at the far end of its gloom. I looked back to the biker, tensed a little and said, "I have a message from Asmodeus."

The nausea hit me almost immediately. Without thinking, I threw myself across the room and behind a set of tables as the two bikers turned towards me with astonishing speed and attempted to grab me. Simultaneously, the bartender swung a shotgun up from somewhere behind the bar and pumped a round into the air where I had been just a few moments before. The noise echoed around the room with an ear-splitting tone as I hit the ground with a grunt, scrabbling to get my footing and dive for the rear exit. I tore down the short corridor and heard literal snarling behind me. I dared not look back, but I could hear scrambling feet and knew that I was being pursued. I slammed into the fire door's release bar at full pelt, throwing the door open and sprawling out into the sunlight; I twisted and fell, going over onto my back. I saw the silhouetted figures of the infernal bikers only a few feet behind me, their eyes glowing ominously red as they reached the doorway. "Ana!" I shouted.

I had barely got the first syllable from my lips when the first biker reached the doorway and leapt out at me, his mouth twisted in a horrendous snarl as he dived. Fortunately that first syllable was all I needed. Anahita appeared in the blink of an eye, catching the diving biker in a roundhouse kick to the face that shifted his direction of travel. He hit the ground with a yowl of pain and rolled a couple of times. The second infernal biker scrabbled at the edge of the doorway to stop his headlong charge out into the sunlight, but apparently demons and angels have to obey the laws of motion as much as anyone else. He tripped over the doorway and reached both hands out to balance himself upon falling. He never got that far. Anahita had him by the throat faster than I could perceive, swung him around and slammed him with such force into the opposite wall of the alleyway that the neighbouring building visibly shuddered. As he sprawled to the ground, I saw Anahita bring up one hand in a swooping motion and smash it down at blistering speed onto the biker's throat. He cried out in utter agony, his scream echoing along the walls of the alley like a police siren. Then he slumped to the ground and was silent.

The other biker was on his feet by now, charging towards Anahita. I shouted a wordless warning at her and she began to turn to meet this new threat. But the other biker was fast, and he was leaping at her before she had time to bring her arms up in defence.

A blast of bright blue light shot past me, as intense as a small star and vibrating the air like a choir of voices. It crashed into the biker like an oncoming truck, abruptly changing his direction and throwing him backwards along the alley at least twenty feet. He bounced several times and lay on the floor, panting.

I saw Alleam step into the alley from the far end, both arms stretched out in front of him, one hand open with palm outwards and the other wrapped around the opposite wrist for stability. He took a few steps forward towards the biker on the floor and calmly said, "Hello, Furcas."

The biker on the floor growled like an animal. "Alleam," he snarled. "I should have known, you duplicitous-"

He never finished the sentence as Alleam hit him with another blast of that ungodly bright light. I squinted and heard Furcas cry out in pain. I looked back up and saw Alleam standing directly over Furcas. "We need some information," Alleam said. "And you're going to oblige, my eternally damned cousin."

Furcas snarled again, glaring at Alleam with an intensity of hatred I had never seen before. "You'll never get away with this," he spat. "This is a direct violation of our treaty rights!"

"I do not speak for the Throne," Alleam said calmly, and then glanced at the entrance to the bar. "And even if I did, your use of illegal outposts would abrogate your protection in this matter."

I groaned, and all three pairs of eyes looked towards me as if they had forgotten I was there. I felt a hand on my wrist and I looked up to see Anahita bent over me, her face covered in concern. "Are you okay?" she asked.

I nodded, accepting her help to stand. "Surprisingly so, yes," I muttered, taking a moment to get my balance. My head throbbed from the adrenaline and my arm hurt horribly from where I had landed on it in the bar. I glared over at Alleam. "What the hell happened to getting him to talk?" I asked angrily. "And who the hell is Asmodeus?"

Furcas growled at the use of the name. Alleam kept his gaze trained on the fallen biker but answered my question. "Asmodeus is a fellow denizen of Hell," he replied calmly. "He and Furcas have an age-old dispute that gets…rather nasty at times."

I blinked. "So you sent me in there knowing that would happen?" I said incredulously.

Alleam glanced at me briefly and then back to Furcas. "It was the only way to get Furcas to act irrationally enough to be lured outside," he elaborated. "Otherwise he would have just killed you outright in the bar."

"So I was bait?" I spat angrily, looking down at Furcas, who gazed back at me with hatred. Another thought struck me. "You said you were trying to keep knowledge of Hell's delegation from me," I said slowly. "And yet you sent me into that place to rile up their third-ranked angel on Earth." I glared at Alleam again. "If I hadn't found out about Hell's presence here earlier, you would have just sent me in there without telling me what was going on?"

Alleam's face flickered with annoyance. "It was necessary to capture him," he said with a tight voice; he was getting angry at all my questions. He folded in his open palm to a fist and pointed one finger at Furcas. A tiny beam of bright light emitted from his fingertip and a pair of simple-looking handcuffs appeared around Furcas' wrists. By the way he glared at them, I doubted they were anywhere near as simple as they looked. "I had to take the chance," he finished quietly.

"You should have told me," a voice said next to me,

shaking in anger. I turned and saw Anahita staring at Alleam with a combination of astonishment and upset; I was genuinely surprised to see her shaking a little with emotion. She stepped forward. "I am this creature's guardian," she said with passion. "That is my role. The meaning of my existence. You should have told me that you were going to throw him into such a dangerous-"

Alleam's gaze snapped to hers and his eyes flared bright blue. Nobody said anything, but I felt the air get incredibly tense for a moment. Anahita went rigid for a moment, before slumping a little in defeat. Feeling my eyes upon her, she quickly straightened her stance and lifted her chin in an attempt at a noble gesture. "My apologies, my Lord," she said in a steady voice. "It is not my place to question."

Alleam nodded slightly. "We need to move fast," he said, drawing himself up to his full height. "The amount of power we have been throwing around is likely to attract attention very soon." He glanced at the bar and smiled slightly. "At least we have put this outpost of Hell out of commission," he said with a slight air of satisfaction.

I smirked. "For someone working against his compatriots, you seem very happy to do them a favour," I remarked with snide.

Alleam's eyes snapped to me and I saw that blue light flare again in his retinas. The air went cold and I got the distinct impression that I had crossed a line. I tensed a little. Alleam spoke calmly, quietly, but I could sense the danger in his voice at pursuing the subject. "I am not a traitor to the Throne," he said, emphasising each word individually. "I do what I must to carry out my holy duties." He looked down his nose at me in a particularly haughty manner. "I also do not need to explain myself to the likes of you," he added derisively. "Just play your role."

I said nothing, but nodded slightly. I had already been

on the receiving end of Alleam's anger and had no wish to repeat the experience. Alleam looked at me for a long moment and then back down to Furcas. "We must go," he said. "I have someone waiting to talk to you." Then he looked back to me. "This will be a little disorientating," he said. "Brace yourself."

I swallowed in apprehension. "Where are we going?" I asked.

Alleam smiled grimly. "To talk to someone who can get the answers we need," he said. Then he clapped his hands together and everything went white.

Chapter 9

I blinked and my eyesight returned.

I was standing with Alleam, Anahita and Furcas in a deserted parking lot, the chipped concrete and faded white lines on the surface showing years of decline and age. Fields stretched out in three directions around us as far as the eye could see. Wherever we were, it was far enough from Chicago that the skyline was not even visible. We were in the shadow of a massive building, a structure of rusting steel and dirtied glass. The faint outline of a company name, indecipherably bleached by the sun, adorned the front above a large entrance. There was nobody in sight and no cars passed by the deserted road behind us. We were in the middle of nowhere.

I swayed a little, my balance affected by the sudden teleportation but not, thankfully, as much as the first time with Anahita. I shook my head and took a couple of deep breaths before looking around to the others and asking, "So, where are we now?"

Alleam did not respond, but merely pursed his lips as he stared up at the building, as if searching for something. I looked over at Anahita and was surprised; her face was twisted in a grimace of fear and her hands were slightly trembling. "Do we have to do this?" she asked, turning to Alleam with a pleading gesture. "Do we really have to involve him again?"

Alleam looked sternly over at Anahita. "It is necessary," he replied. "You know this is the only way to discover the information we need."

I was suddenly apprehensive; I did not know what kind of person could make an angel visibly tremble with fear, but I doubted they were somebody of whom I wanted to be on the wrong side. I glanced at Furcas; he seemed to be as confused and apprehensive about the situation as I was; although, I got the impression this was going to turn out much worse for him. I was just opening my mouth to ask one of the hundreds of questions I had when I heard a shout from the building's entrance. I turned and squinted through the bright sunlight.

A man with long hair and an open, loose fitting shirt was waving at us from the entrance way. "Welcome!" he shouted, a beaming smile across his face. "Please, come inside."

I blinked, a little taken aback. Alleam stepped forward, pushing Furcas in front of him. Anahita followed, still looking like she would rather be anywhere else. I followed in her wake, my eyes flitting from window to window, searching for potential danger. Alleam climbed the steps to the front entrance and stopped before the man, bowing his head a little. "My greetings to you, Warden," he said with diplomatic courtesy.

The man bowed his head in return. "And to you, my Lord Principal," he said with reverence. Then his eyes flicked to Furcas. "Another necessity?" he asked with a slight air of weariness. "It is most exhausting for him."

Alleam nodded grimly in response. "Another necessity," he confirmed. "Please, announce us to him."

The man nodded again and then turned to myself and Anahita. He bowed his head to both of us in turn and smiled. "Our community welcomes you all," he said, and stretched his hand back towards the corridor behind him. "Please, follow me," he added.

We followed him along the corridor and deeper into the building. The rooms on the ground floor appeared to be deserted, dilapidated and decaying office furniture lining the walls. But then, as we climbed the dingy stairwell to the next floor up, we were suddenly in the company of scores of people. Children ran along the corridor, laughing and playing with each other as we passed by. I looked into the adjoining rooms, seeing dozens of people at a time engaged in daily life. One room had been equipped into some kind of manufacturing set-up, with people leaning over lathes and electric saws and other tools as they worked on various items; I saw one man fitting together a table, whilst two women worked on what appeared to be a disassembled engine of some kind. In another room I saw children reading quietly whilst a man stood in front of a large whiteboard, its surface filled with notes on literature and philosophy. Another room was filled with bunk beds, whilst yet another appeared to be fully set up as an infirmary. I was completely astonished by what I was seeing. "What is this place?" I asked, looking over at our guide.

The man smiled, glancing over his shoulder at me as we continued to walk. "This is a community," he said. "Brought together in the spirit of harmony and co-operation. We are almost completely self-sufficient here; our gardens cater for all of our food needs. We even have a doctor living with us." We turned into another corridor that was lined with several more workshops, their inhabitants all repairing or manufacturing something. "What we cannot produce ourselves," the man continued, "we swap for the skills of our inhabitants with nearby communities. We live in peace and we harm nobody."

I nodded as he spoke, still completely astounded by the full and vibrant community that was living within the shell of this forgotten, isolated office block. I turned to say something to Anahita, but stopped when I saw that she still looked incredibly troubled. Her eyes flicked from one room to another as if expecting something to jump out at any moment. She walked rigidly, each step a labour to accomplish. I stepped up next to her and said in a low voice, "What's wrong? This all seems to be quite safe."

Anahita looked at me briefly, her lips pursed. "It's not

where we are," she said with an air of reluctance. "It is who we are here to see."

I raised my eyebrows in surprise. "You're an angel," I pointed out. "What could possibly be so bad as to scare you?"

Anahita glanced at me sidelong with a slight, weary smile. "Everyone is scared of a person that can see straight through them," she said.

I did not know how to respond to that. Anahita went back to watching her surroundings in the same nervous manner she had before. I stayed silent and followed the group up several more flights of stairs, past more rooms vibrant with activity, wondering who exactly I was about to meet.

Our guide eventually paused outside a door that had once read 'Managing Director', now little more than a faded outline. The frosted glass in the window prevented us from seeing through to the other side. He knocked three times quietly. A muffled voice called from inside and he opened the door and stood to one side, inviting us to enter first. Alleam led us inside.

The room was spartan; it had been cleared of its previous furniture and several slightly lighter areas of the carpet told us where they had stood. The walls were bare apart from a clock and two shelves lined with religious and philosophical texts. A large, floor-to-ceiling window at the far end of the room led onto a balcony overlooking the rear of the building. I could see more fields stretching away into the distance and movements of people on the land; the gardens that our guide had mentioned, I surmised. There was a mattress in one corner, and on that mattress sat a man.

Even when seated cross-legged with his back slightly stooped, I could tell he was a tall man. He had long, blonde hair that almost reached his waist. His skin was pale and complimented the loose, white cotton shirt and trousers that he wore. His eyes were closed and his palms were rested on his crossed knees. I was struck with how peaceful he looked and had the sudden, inexplicable urge to sit on the floor myself and join him. Without any cue and yet knowing to do so, we all stood in silence and waited.

After a moment, the man opened his eyes slowly. He smiled and rubbed his face gently, as if he had just awoken from a light sleep. Alleam bowed his head in respect but said nothing. The man's eyes rested upon Alleam and the smile broke into a broad grin, as if seeing an age-old friend for the first time in ages. He stood slowly, stretching a little as he did, and then walked across to Alleam. He clasped both hands down on his shoulders and embraced the angel in a tight hug. Alleam looked a little taken aback by the intimate gesture but, after a moment, returned the embrace gently. After a moment, the man pulled back from Alleam and his face had changed to one of sympathy. "You carry a heavy load, my friend," he suddenly spoke. His voice was deep and gentle, echoing around the room with perfect clarity despite the low volume. "You still have a long way to go," he added, patting Alleam on both shoulders gently. "Have strength, my brother."

Alleam nodded in response. "I will see this through, as I promised," he said.

The man nodded in reply. "I know you will," he said, and patted Alleam on the shoulder once more. Then he turned to Anahita. My guardian angel was studying the floor, refusing to look up at anything else. The man reached out and gently touched her shoulder. She did not flinch away, but nor did she acknowledge the gesture as pleasant. The man smiled a little sadly and lowered his hand to his side. Then he turned to me and his eyes widened in surprise. He opened his mouth to speak, and then closed it again. I watched him study me for a moment, before glancing at Alleam. The angel said nothing, his face entirely neutral. The man then looked back to me and smiled again, reaching out a hand. "I bid you greetings, my friend," he said. "My name is Norman."

I looked down at the hand warily, but something in my gut reassured me that I was safe. I slowly reached out a hand in response and took his. It was warm, like mine. I shook it. "Sam," I responded. And then, unable to stop myself, I asked, "What are you?"

Norman looked me in the eyes for a while before shrugging slightly. "A means to an end," he said simply, smiling at me still. "As we all are, in the grand scheme of things."

Alleam cleared his throat and Norman's attention shifted to the angel. "You know why we are here?" Alleam asked. Norman merely quirked a slight smile and Alleam tilted his head in acknowledgement. "Of course you do," he corrected, and then turned to Furcas. "This is the one in question," he said.

Norman turned to look at Furcas, who was staring warily in return. "Must it be done?" Norman asked, a noticeable twinge of tiredness and regret in his voice.

Alleam nodded. "I am afraid so," he said. He pushed Furcas forward a few more steps. "He has information that we must have."

Norman stepped up to Furcas, who jutted out his jaw in a defiant manner. "And what are you going to do?" the fallen sneered, eyeing the other man up and down. "Give me a hug and tell me it's all going to be okay?"

Norman looked Furcas in the eye with no change in expression, as if Furcas had not even spoken. He reached out one hand and touched the side of the infernal biker's face. To my utter astonishment, I saw Furcas go weak at the knees and nearly buckle under his own weight. The cocksure expression on the biker's face disappeared to be replaced with one of confusion and – yes, most definitely – fear. "What are you-?" he whispered, trailing off without finishing the sentence.

Norman sighed, his brow furrowed and his lips pursed. "You have done much to hurt others," he said softly, looking deep into Furcas' eyes. "And yet, you burn with pain yourself; your very essence is laced with torment." Norman shook his head slowly. "The world would be a much nicer place if everyone could see the pain inside others," he said softly. Then he looked back to Alleam. "No other options?" he asked.

Alleam shook his head. "No other options," he echoed, looking down at Furcas.

Norman sighed again and turned back to the biker in front of him. He smiled apologetically. "I'm sorry." he said, and brought his free hand up to clasp the other side of Furcas' face.

It is difficult for me to describe what happened next because I could see very little of it. As soon as Norman touched Furcas with both hands, cradling the biker's face in his palms, there was a tremendous roar of noise, as if a massive wave was crashing down upon us. Norman and Furcas were enveloped in a blinding white light that illuminated the room like a star, causing me to turn my head away and shield my eyes from the glare. Even through my eyelids the light burned and I clasped my hands to my face for further protection. Above the roaring I heard a wailing noise and I realised after a moment that it was Furcas. It was a piercing, baleful noise of somebody in agony and somehow I understood that it was not physical but mental, as if someone was being subjected to all their worst memories and nightmares simultaneously. I wanted to cover my ears but the light forced me to keep my hands over my face, and I gritted my teeth to help deal with the noise.

When the light finally faded, I was disoriented and trembling. I lowered my hands slowly and blinked a few times.

For a moment I could not see and panicked, but realised that the darkness in my eyes was simply the after image of the light and that it was gradually fading. I felt like I had been standing there for an hour, but one look at the clock told me that it had only been a few minutes since we had entered the room. I looked around; Alleam was standing motionless, his expression unchanged from before the event. Anahita, in contrast, was trembling even more than before; she had not closed her eyes, but she had turned away. I looked across at Norman, who had broken contact with Furcas and had moved a few steps away. Furcas himself was slumped on the floor and breathing heavily. Blackened scorch marks lined both sides of his face in the shape of Norman's hands. The room felt deathly silent after all the noise.

Norman turned to Alleam. His face still held the same serenity that it had before but he looked substantially more tired. "I have what you require," he said. "I must speak with you alone."

Alleam nodded and turned to myself and Anahita. "Step outside," he ordered softly.

Still completely unnerved by what had just happened, I did so without question or comment. Anahita followed after me. The door closed behind us and we found ourselves alone in the corridor outside the office. The sound of children laughing on the floor below us echoed up the nearby stairwell, as did the noise of tools and equipment from the workshops below us. It was disorientating to move from the one situation to the other and I slumped against the wall and took a few moments to breathe deeply. "What just happened in there?" I asked.

Anahita did not answer at first. I looked up and saw an expression of distant sadness on her face. "A sifting of the mind," she said quietly, not quite meeting my eyes. "A searching of the brain for information and the extraction of what was needed."

I looked at her for a moment, letting everything sink in. "Norman is one of you, isn't he?" I asked.

Anahita looked up sharply as if I had just said something insulting. Seeing no such intent on my face, she relaxed her stance a little and nodded. "In a way," she said. "Norman is a fallen angel."

I rubbed my forehead. "So he's Hell-oriented," I concluded.

Anahita shook her head briefly. "No, he's…" she said, and petered out. "It's complicated to explain," she said.

I looked up at her with a tired expression. "To call this entire situation complicated would be the understatement of the century," I said wearily. "I haven't been reduced to a gibbering wreck by anything yet, so please; enlighten me."

Anahita sighed and leaned against the wall opposite me. Using it to support her back, she slid down until she was sitting on her haunches close to the floor. She looked tired. I followed suit and we sat opposite each other in silence for a couple of minutes before she began to speak. "A long time ago," she explained. "There was a rebellion in Heaven; one that led to a number of angels leaving."

I nodded. "Lucifer's rebellion," I acknowledged.

To my surprise, Anahita shook her head. "Before that," she said. "When humanity was first cast out of the Garden of Eden and began to spread across the world. There were a number of angels who questioned the wisdom of God and the way in which the angels were required to be apart from humanity. We call them The First Fallen, and they left Heaven to take husbands and wives amongst the human population." Anahita glanced up at me. "That's where most Elioud bloodlines started from," she elaborated.

I nodded to myself. "And Norman was one of The First Fallen?" I asked.

Anahita nodded. "Him and many others," she said. "They were shamed and declared traitors and heretics. God attempted to wipe them out along with large swathes of humanity that they had come into contact with; you know this through the tale of Noah and the Great Flood." Anahita looked down at her feet for a moment. "It did not get everyone," she continued. "Norman was one who managed to survive."

"And this mind sift ability of his," I reflected. "This is something that angels can do?"

"A very small number can, yes," Anahita said. "There were once many more, but the majority left with the exodus of The First Fallen and were subsequently killed." She placed both hands on the floor and guided herself down into a seated position, stretching out her legs with evident relief. I was constantly struck with how many human gestures I was noticing within the angels that I had come into contact with. "Between that and Lucifer's subsequent rebellion, it has taken centuries for the Throne to build its powers back up to a comparative level to those early days," she continued. "And even then, we have nobody as strong in what they do as Norman."

I looked up and down the corridor. "So he's hiding here?" I asked. "He's set himself up a little cult of worshippers and keeping his head down?"

Anahita looked up at me with a scornful look. "These are not his worshippers," she said tersely. "These are the people he protects. He is their confidante, their counsellor and their defender. He is the guardian angel of all who live here; all of those who do not identify with the world as it currently works." She looked back at the floor. "He is a good man," she concluded quietly.

I wanted to ask her why she was so uncomfortable around Norman, but I felt that I would likely be pushing too far with such an intimate question. So instead I cleared my throat and said, "I never thanked you for saving me from Furcas and his fallen angel friend earlier on."

Anahita smiled a little at my comment. "It is my role," she said by way of acknowledgement.

I leant across the corridor and put my hand on one of hers. She looked up in surprise at the gesture. "That doesn't mean it isn't appreciated," I said sincerely. "Thank you."

Anahita opened her mouth to say something, and then closed it again. She looked thoroughly dumbfounded by my comment. She went to speak again, but was interrupted by the opening of the office door. We both sprang to our feet as Alleam stepped out into the corridor, dragging an unconscious Furcas behind him. Alleam looked at Anahita and nodded. "We have the information we need," he said. Then he turned to me and said, "Norman wants to speak to you alone."

I glanced at the office door, rather apprehensive about stepping back through. Alleam saw my worry and his tone became a little softer. "You're safe in there," he said. "We'll be waiting outside." And with that, he and Anahita continued along the corridor, dragging Furcas behind them by the arms.

I turned to the door and wondered momentarily if I should knock. I shook my head at the ridiculousness of that thought given the current circumstances and opened the door. I stepped inside the office and, with much reluctance, let the door swing closed behind me.

Norman was standing at the far end of the room, looking out of the floor-length window onto the fields outside. The sun was gradually sliding into the late afternoon and cast a golden glow across the people working the land, gathering and planting the crops that helped to sustain this community. Norman had his back to me and did not immediately move as I entered. We stood there in silence for a few minutes, the only sound being the clock ticking on the wall. Then Norman asked, "What year is it?"

I was a little taken aback by the question, but I told him anyway. Norman turned from the window to look at me, a gentle smile on his face. "I have difficulty understanding time," he said, walking across the room towards me. "I have seen buildings rise and fall beyond this window and I have seen civilisations do the same from much higher, but to me it all seems near-instantaneous." He looked down at the mattress. "I once sat down to meditate and my Wardens told me afterwards that I had not moved a muscle for six months." He smiled, and shook his head. "What a funny thing time is," he observed. "You humans have so little, and yet you only realise that when there's hardly any left."

I got up the courage to speak. "So, you're thousands of years old?" I asked.

Norman looked up at me again and thought for a moment. "Yes and no," he replied. "I live, and yet this body withers and dies and is replaced with another. A reincarnation of the soul, I suppose. It happens to all of us angels that live on Earth for long periods of time."

"And what you did to Furcas was some kind of mind reading?" I asked.

Norman nodded. "In a way," he agreed. "I empathise with people; I understand them on a very basic and emotional level. Being able to access direct memories is merely an extreme version of that ability." His smile faltered a little. "I do not enjoy it," he concluded, his voice a little softer than before.

"So why do you do it?" I asked, and immediately regretting the personal way that could have been taken.

Norman merely smiled at me. "Because it is my job," he said, and then inclined his head in a thoughtful manner.

"Was my job," he corrected himself. "And despite not wanting that to be my job anymore, it is still sometimes necessary to protect those around me."

I mused this for a moment. "You understand me just by looking?" I asked.

Norman nodded. He walked towards me until he was only a few feet away. "You're unique, Samuel," he said.

I smirked despite my unease. "Flattery will get you nowhere," I remarked.

Norman cocked his head, as if he did not quite understand. "There is much you have not been told yet," he remarked. "You have more connection to Alleam's goals than you realise."

I frowned. "How so?" I asked.

Norman smiled. "You have the ability to be much more powerful than you currently are," he said, placing his hand on my shoulder. The gesture was remarkably comforting and almost immediately I felt more at ease. "There will be people you meet who will encourage you to develop your powers. What is important is the motivation behind the use of those powers." Norman squeezed my shoulder a little in a supportive way. "Tread carefully, my friend," he said with genuine concern.

And then he frowned. He reached up to the side of my face. I flinched a little and Norman paused for a moment. "It's okay," he said with a smile, and I believed him. Norman gently touched the side of my face and I felt a surge of warmth rush through my skin that made me gasp. I felt my knees buckle slightly and I reached out to support myself on his shoulder. A great rush of pleasant feeling poured through my body like water and when Norman finally broke contact, I felt like I had just slept for a day. "Wow," I murmured to myself. "What was that?"

Norman did not answer, but frowned in a puzzled way.

"Somebody has been inside your mind," he remarked.

I looked up sharply, my feelings of reassurance being replaced with a rush of alarm. "What do you mean?" I asked.

Norman shook his head slowly. "I'm not quite sure," he said carefully, scrutinising me closely. "But you should be careful about your company whilst I work it out." Then he smiled again. "We will meet again soon, Sam," he said, turning away from me to look back at the window. "If not in this life, then perhaps the next." He then went silent, observing the sun setting on the people working the fields outside.

I stood there for a moment, unsure if I should ask any further questions but fairly sure I would get no further answers. Eventually I turned and quietly left, leaving Norman in the silence of his room.

I was incredibly confused. This entire situation just seemed to be getting deeper with every day I was involved, and for every question I had answered there were several follow-ups to which I did not have the answer. Norman's comments on somebody in my mind were particularly alarming, but he had been vague on the specifics of what that meant. I believed that he wanted to tell me more but got the impression that something was stopping him from doing so. Alleam perhaps, or some external circumstances I was not aware of yet. I rubbed my face, leaning against the stairwell wall for a moment and tried to balance my thoughts. It felt like I was fighting somebody blindfolded with both hands tied. I needed more information and I needed it soon.

There was a window in the stairwell and I could see out onto the front parking lot where we had begun. I saw Alleam and Anahita, with Furcas still unconscious at their feet. They were talking…actually, as I leaned into the window a little further, I realised that they were arguing. I frowned, wondering what was going on. And then I remembered being in the biker complex with Gemma, and her soft voice close to my face. "Just close your eyes and imagine that you're looking through a window," she had said. Then she had smiled. I had liked that smile.

I closed my eyes, took several deep breaths and visualised. It was easier given that I had a literal window this time, and the sudden rush of extra-bodily movement came quicker than previously. I felt myself lifting from my body and moving, through the wall and out into the blazing sunlight of the late afternoon, slowly descending towards the ground and landing softly nearby where Anahita and Alleam were standing.

"...dare you go against my wishes!" Alleam was shouting at Anahita. His face was twisted with anger, the strongest emotional response I had seen out of him so far. He was literally shaking with rage. "I gave you explicit instructions to keep information about Norman to a minimum and then you go and tell him the entire story?"

"I did not tell him the entire story!" Anahita shouted back. She was trembling with fear at the stronger, higher-ranked angel in front of her, but she was refusing to back down. "There is a massive amount he does not yet know and I agree that we should keep him away from that. But he has to have some information or he is dead already!" She shook her head bitterly. "It is bad enough that you sent him into the bar without telling him what he was getting into, let alone be irresponsible enough not to tell his guardian angel that you were-"

She recoiled suddenly, as if physically slapped. I felt a wave of energy that threatened to knock me over and had to take a step back. Alleam had thrown an arm out and had his palm stretched out towards Anahita. His eyes were a blazing blue and his face was full of anger. "I am an angel of the Lord," he thundered. "I am a member of the Principal Choir. I have seen empires rise and fall. I have guided nations and peoples through triumph and adversity. I will not be lectured by the likes of you." He shook his head with a despairing smile. "You do understand what is going on, right?" he asked. "We are dealing with the Apocalypse, the very End of Days. There is no time for sentimentality or second-guessing, and there is certainly no leeway in our plans when it comes to him." The blaze began to fade from his eyes and his voice became calmer. "You will follow the plan as specified or you will leave my protection and take your chances with the agents of the Throne, is that clear?"

Anahita looked utterly shocked by what had just happened. She opened her mouth and closed it a couple of times. Then she merely nodded and lowered her head. "I understand," she said quietly.

"Good." Alleam's eyes had faded back to normal now. "We have to move fast with this information and I need you ready to do your duty." He glanced up towards the building. "We need to get moving," he added. "Go find Sam."

Anahita nodded and turned back towards the building. I let go of the image and felt myself rushing back towards the building until I was back in my own body. I opened my eyes and gasped, taking a couple of deep breaths to deal with the dizzying after effects of the viewing. I began to hurry down the stairs, aware that Anahita was looking for me.

I reflected on what I had seen as I descended the stairs. Norman was right; there was a lot more going on here than I was being made aware of. I was being kept purposefully in the dark for reasons I could not fathom, and the frustration of that was starting to get to me. I hated working in the dark; it went against everything I knew as a detective. If I was not careful, these people – these *creatures* - would get me killed.

I met Anahita at the bottom of the stairs. She had recovered herself by now and looked the epitome of the calm protector. I almost ran into her and she inclined her head towards the door. "We're ready to go," she said, and then paused. "What did he say to you?" she asked, frowning.

I thought for a moment. "Not enough," I said, "But enough to be useful."

Anahita quirked a slight smile. "That is pretty normal for him," she said. "Come on, we have to go." And with that, we turned and stepped out into the sunlight.

Chapter 10

I was running.

I was on the shore of a lake, running parallel to its crystal blue waters. The sand was warm beneath my feet and the sun shone down on me from above. I barely noticed any of these things as my legs pounded as fast as they could, my heart beating frantically as I prayed they were not catching up to me.

They were. I heard the gallop of horses over my shoulder and I turned to see my pursuers charging towards me, their blue uniforms distinct even at this distance. Both of them had swords raised above their heads as they turned onto the sand and bore down on me, the hooves of their steeds kicking up great plumes of sand in their wake as they charged. I was never going to outrun them like this, but I refused to be taken so easily.

I passed an outcrop of rocks on the beach, counted a few paces in my head, and then turned and flung my hands out towards them, willing them to move with the powers at my disposal. Several of the rocks, some the size of a human skull, lifted from the sand and flew at high speed towards my pursuers. The largest caught one of my pursuers square in the jaw and sent him flying from his horse and into the sand. The other managed to evade the flying obstacles and continued to close on me. He would be in striking range within moments.

I was utterly exhausted. I pushed as much energy into my legs as I could, but my muscles were weakening by the moment. There was no way I could escape. Eventually I stumbled, as I already knew that I would, and fell to my knees at the water's edge, panting hard. The face of a Native American stared back at me. I did not understand, but I had little time to wonder. I heard a cry behind me and turned, seeing the horseman upon me. His sabre was raised above his head and he snarled some kind of curse at me. I put my hands up to protect myself, but to no avail. The sabre fell through the air, and I saw the Native American's panicked expression in its reflection.

☦

I woke up, covered in sweat, my heart still pounding from the imagined exertion. I still saw the sabre falling in the after-image of my mind, imprinted against the darkness to which I awoke. I blinked a couple of times and let my eyes adjust.

I was lying on the bed in the same cheap motel that I had stayed at the previous night. I had been left there by Alleam after he had teleported us back from our meeting with Norman; I was still too worried to go anywhere near either my apartment or my office without arousing the attention of any potential watchers or attackers that may be lurking nearby. Alleam had handed me a pre-paid cell phone and had told me to wait for further instructions; then he had teleported away with Anahita and Furcas in tow. I got the impression from Anahita that Furcas would be unceremoniously dumped outside the Hell delegation's compound; nobody would follow it up because of the potential revelations of treaty breaking by Hell and Furcas would be punished internally for letting himself get caught whilst engaged in what basically amounted to espionage. I had drunk a third of a bottle of whisky and managed to lapse into unconsciousness. The dreaming had started almost immediately.

I looked over at the clock on the table, which told me it as just past three in morning. I sighed, stretching out on the bed and staring at the ceiling. My head was swimming with the tail end of the whisky and the beginnings of a hangover. The room was deathly silent, barely any traffic noise outside. I was tired, confused and alone.

I reflected on that last part; this was not the first time I had been on my own facing a hostile situation. Many times in my early life I had been required to defend myself against somebody bigger, faster, or more intelligent than me. It was that very struggle that gave me the attentive eye I have today, and I had used that skill to stay aware of my situation whenever possible and kept myself one step ahead of those trying to do me harm.

This situation was beyond anything I could have imagined. I was trapped between three factions of honest-to-God literal angels, at least two of which were out to kill me and I barely trusted the third. All because I was stuck with abilities I neither enjoyed nor wished to have, despite their benefit of keeping me alive on occasion. I felt the overwhelming urge to curl into a foetal position and try to forget everything that had happened in the last few days. Instead, I forced myself to stand; trying to hide from the world would solve none of these issues.

I padded to the little bathroom and filled a glass with water from the tap. I took a long draw from it and leaned against the sink, trying to collect my thoughts.

There was something big that I was not being told; that much was evident. The argument between Alleam and Anahita had really brought that home for me, and I wondered what major element I was being kept in the dark about. I had also been shaken by how furious Alleam had become with Anahita at the time; I had started becoming accustomed to seeing these angels as near-emotionless aliens that had little interest in the world they were professing to protect. That had distinctly changed yesterday; I was dealing with highly emotional and dangerous individuals that had the added bonus of being powerful enough to end the world. And apparently the ones I had met so far were nowhere near the most powerful; I reflected on the scale of power I had seen in Norman.

I suddenly felt a brief wave of nausea pass over me, and steadied myself against the sink. I sighed, shaking my head a little, and turned to walk back into the bedroom. I sat myself back down on the bed and took another sip of my water. Then I placed the glass down on the side table, leaned forward to focus on it closely, and said, "How long have you been there?"

I heard Gemma jump. She had been crouched in the corner; I had not noticed her initially, but my Sight had let me know about her presence whilst I had been in the bathroom. I looked directly at her to make sure she knew that I was aware of her presence; she was sitting with her back to the wall and her legs drawn up to her chest. She stared at me through the low gloom and smiled slightly. "You're getting better at dealing with that," she said.

I sighed, leaning back in the couch and rubbed my eyes a little. "I've had a lot of practice recently," I remarked, then looked back over to her. "What are you doing here?" I asked.

Gemma shrugged; she looked small and alone. "I didn't have anywhere else to go," she said quietly.

I grunted. "So you were just going to sit there all night?" I asked.

She shrugged again. "I didn't want to wake you," she replied.

I sighed, reaching for my water again. "So why do you have nowhere to go?" I asked.

Gemma sighed. "I was staying with some of the other Elioud from the network," she said, stretching her legs out with an audible noise of satisfaction. "They got angry at me for the rampage I went on during our escape from the compound; they were worried about the potential exposure of me and others to the angels." She studied her feet closely. "They've excommunicated me until they work out what they want to do with me in the long-run."

I looked at her for a long moment. All the bravado I had previously seen within her was gone; the cocky, risk-taking thrill-seeker that had helped me bust into and out of a biker compound had been replaced by a sad, frightened woman with nowhere to go. I felt sorry for her and my expression softened. "You can crash here tonight," I said, nodding to the little fold-out sofa along one wall. "If you're going to go to the trouble of sneaking in here, you might as well be comfortable."

I saw Gemma smile despite the low light. "Thank you," she said softly.

I nodded. "Don't mention it," I replied, glancing again at the clock. My stomach growled and I suddenly realised how long it had been since I had eaten a proper meal. "Are you hungry?" I asked Gemma. She nodded. I climbed off the bed again and went to grab my jacket. "Come on," I said. "There's a place around the corner."

☦

The 24-hour diner was as cheap and dishevelled as the motel, but the food smelled delicious in an utterly artery-clogging way. We grabbed a booth seat and ordered from a bored-looking waitress. As she disappeared to get food and coffee, Gemma looked at me across the table with an anxious expression and said, "I'm sorry for any trouble I've caused you."

I laughed, leaning back in the booth's plush seats and shaking my head. "I think trouble is probably putting it lightly," I replied. Then I saw the anxiety turn to sadness and I felt sorry for what I said. "It's okay," I said, smiling sympathetically at her. "You saved my life just as much as you put it in jeopardy. I've got a lot of people trying to cause me trouble right now; at least you've been one of the more honest people about everything so far."

The waitress arrived with two mugs of steaming coffee and we spent a moment savouring their warmth. There was a television in the corner of the diner and I turned to pay attention to it momentarily. It was a repeat of a late-night talk show that I had seen sometime last week; the overly-jovial host was interviewing Francis Bowman, the Vice-President of the United States. I watched the grandfatherly-looking statesman lean forward in the chair and smile politely. "There are many challenges ahead in the America of today," Bowman's deep, southern accent spilled from the speakers. "The decline in moral standards across our great nation is a threat to society and a threat to security. It must be addressed and it must be reversed before the worst happens."

I grunted to myself. "Little too late, buddy," I muttered, taking a sip of the coffee. I looked back to Gemma, who was savouring hers as if it was water in the desert. I watched her for a moment. "So how come you don't have a home to go to?" I asked.

Gemma swallowed a mouthful of coffee slowly as she thought about how to respond. "Having abilities like we do," she began, and then she sighed. "It's a bit of a social problem; we often…don't get on well with others." She shrugged and sipped her coffee. "And that's just the well-adjusted Elioud," she added. "You're definitely the most stable out of any I have ever met."

I frowned. "Why's that?" I asked.

The food arrived; a couple of simple sandwiches that had not taken long to make. Gemma took a moment to begin eating before she answered my question. "Most Elioud find their powers difficult to control," she said. "They cannot comprehend why they are different, which leads many of them to be pushed to the boundaries of society. You see them on the street sometimes, ranting about how they can read thoughts or see the future."

I raised an eyebrow. "So all those people I've thought are just mentally ill are actually descended from angels?" I asked dubiously, taking up my own sandwich in one hand and biting into it.

Gemma shook her head. "Not all of them; some are just people with psychological issues." She quirked a slight smile. "But there are more than you think out there with some angel in their blood." She took another bite of her sandwich. "That's part of what the Elioud network does; those of us who are more stable look after those who are not in a position to do so themselves."

I was about to reply when I was suddenly struck with a wave of nausea just as a waitress walked by our table. Instinctively, I turned in my seat and reached out an arm just as the waitress tripped – as I had known she would – over a shoelace that she had not properly tied. I managed to catch her in the crook of my arm as she fell and she blinked in confusion. "Are you okay?" I asked.

She nodded with a weary smile. "Yeah, just a little tired," she replied, regaining her balance. "Thank you," she added, before walking across to the nearby chair to fix her shoe.

I turned back to the table to see Gemma staring at me in fascination. "Did you see that about to happen?" she asked.

I nodded reluctantly, glancing around the diner. A few onlookers were glancing in our direction curiously following what just happened. "Yeah," I said quietly. "It's a useful but rather awkward ability to have sometimes."

Gemma leaned back in her chair, blowing air from her cheeks in an impressed way. "This is remarkable," she said.

I shrugged. "Surely you must see that sort of thing all the time with other Elioud." I remarked.

Gemma shook her head. "Actually no," she replied. "You're pretty special, Sam."

I raised an eyebrow. "Flattery will get you nowhere," I remarked, lifting the coffee cup to my lips again.

Gemma smirked a little. "No, dummy; listen," and she leant forward on the table and started counting off on her fingers. "Angelic powers fall into four categories," she explained. "Those are telepathy, precognition, clairvoyance and psychokinesis."

I looked at her blankly. "In English, please," I replied.

Gemma rolled her eyes at me. "Alright, big print version," she said. "Most angels are psychokinetic, which means abilities to fly, move things around, and in the most powerful cases to directly manipulate and change matter; bring down fire and brimstone, that sort of thing. Then you've got telepaths who can read thoughts; precognicists who can foretell the future; and clairvoyants who can obtain information about places or events at remote locations." She reached for her coffee again. "These other three categories of angel are much rarer and they tend to be employed as specialists." She looked at me with a quizzical expression. "Which makes you even stranger."

"How so?" I asked.

Gemma held up two fingers. "Well, I've seen you exercise clairvoyant powers before, when you watched Banniel and Astartoth square off at each-other during their meeting," she observed. "Now I've just seen you exercise powers of precognition as well, stopping that waitress from tripping and hurting herself." She leaned forward. "In the distant past, it's said that all angels used to be have the ability to use all four power types. After the rebellion by Lucifer, God split the powers of the remaining loyal angels into different groups to prevent individual angels from having any more power than the rest, also making future rebellion harder. Clairvoyants in particular are very rare in the Heavenly camp nowadays; most of them left with the Rebellion." Gemma looked at me with a fascinated expression. "That you can manifest two out of four of those powers from your ancestors is incredibly rare."

I studied my cup for a while. "How do you control your powers?" I asked after a moment. "You're a psychokinetic, right?"

Gemma nodded. "Mostly physical manipulation of objects," she clarified. "No summoning fire or energy out of thin air for me, but what I can do is more than enough to protect myself." She sighed, trying to think an answer. "You just sort of – it's hard to describe- you just sort of focus on what you want to happen in your mind's eye and let it happen." She shrugged with a slight smile. "It's the best way I can describe it," she added.

"No, I think I understand," I replied, eating the last of my sandwich. "It's like when you told me to focus on where I wanted to be looking during the meeting at the compound."

Gemma smiled. "Exactly like that," she agreed. "It takes some time and discipline to control it, but that's the essence of it. You just have to accept your ability to do what you're imagining you can do; as if you were simply extending a limb."

We finished our food and left the diner, heading back to the motel. The evening had grown cooler and I offered Gemma my jacket to keep her warm. She accepted it graciously and slipped an arm around my own as we walked. There was an instant tension in the air that had not been there a few minutes before as I tried to work out what I should say next.

I did not have much time to dwell before fate decided to step in. As we turned down the street leading to the motel, a couple of men stepped out of the shadows towards us. Both were dishevelled and unshaven and had a desperate look in their eyes. One of them walked right up to me and jabbed a finger in my face. "Give me your wallet and nobody gets hurt," he said in a low voice.

I froze in place, trying to think what to do next. Gemma was standing very still next to me. "Okay buddy," I said, reaching out my free hand with my palm out in a gesture of submission. "Take it easy and I'll get you what money I have."

"Are you deaf?" the man spat at me, one hand in his pocket quite conspicuously. "I said the entire wallet; now hand it over."

I sighed. "Look buddy, there's nothing you can do with the few cards I've got; it's just going to cause me inconvenience. Now, if you'll just-"

The dizziness hit me. I staggered half a step but recovered quickly; certainly in time enough to swing myself and Gemma out of the way of the man's hand as it swung from his pocket, a blade glinting in his grasp. It missed us by a few inches and the attacker stumbled a little, not expecting to meet thin air with his swing. Acting quickly, I spun around and kicked the man in his leg, sending him crashing to the floor with a howl of pain. I saw the other man charging at me from the corner of my eye and began to turn to meet him. Before I could, a trash can slammed into the man at torso height, knocking him sideways. He landed against the wall with a grunt and slid down it with a groan of pain. I turned and saw Gemma with both hands out-stretched like a conductor, directing the trash can in its flight. The two men scrambled to their feet and began running in the opposite direction, clearly terrified of what they had just witnessed.

Gemma walked back across to me and we grinned at each-other, panting heavily from the exertion. "That was fun," she said between gasps.

"Yeah, it was," I agreed, and to my surprise I found that I meant it. Despite the life-threatening situation, I had genuinely actually enjoyed using my abilities for something, possibly for the first time in my life. It made me feel good to know that we had potentially put those two off from attacking again, at least for a little while. "You know," I said, turning to Gemma. "With outcomes like that, I could get used to knowing what people are about to do next."

Gemma grinned. "I bet you didn't foretell this," she said.

And then she kissed me.

Chapter 11

When I woke the next morning, she was gone.

I was back in the motel room, lying in the middle of a set of dishevelled sheets. Gemma's kiss had taken me by surprise, but I had adapted rather quickly to the situation. We fell asleep in each-other's arms, tired and exorcised of the stress of the last few days. Being alone in the bed was the first thing I noticed when I regained consciousness. The second thing was the knocking at the door.

I slipped out of bed quietly, reaching for the nearest heavy object I could find. I sorely wished I had my gun with me, but it was still in my office drawer. Picking up the lamp, I quietly walked over to the door and glanced through the peephole. A man in a black suit with dark sunglasses stood motionlessly in front of the door, his face set in a grim expression. I unlocked the door and opened it a few inches, keeping the lamp just out of sight. "Yeah?" I said carefully.

The man looked at me for a long moment from behind those sunglasses. "Samuel?" he asked in a brisk, businesslike manner.

"Who wants to know?" I said, my hand tightening around the lamp in case I needed to swing it quickly. Hopefully this guy was not carrying a firearm; if he was, then I was pretty much dead.

The man reached into his pocket and I flinched slightly. He must have noticed, because he removed his hand more slowly. He flipped open a leather case that displayed his identification. "Secret Service, sir," he said. "My name is Agent Daniels. I'd like to ask you a few questions."

There was a table by the door, and I placed the lamp gently down on it just out of the man's eyeshot. "What does the Secret Service want with me?" I asked cautiously.

Daniels barely changed his expression. "Why are you checking information on one of our vehicles in the Presidential protection detail?" he demanded.

I blinked; I remembered that Jim had said he needed to push my enquiry up to his superiors regarding the government car in the biker compound. He had promised to try to keep my name out of things, but obviously that had not been possible. "It's pertinent to a case that I'm investigating," I replied, staring Daniels straight in the eyes. I could see nothing behind those sunglasses and found myself looking back at my own reflection. I looked like hell.

Daniels pushed open the door and forced me to step back. He took a few steps into the motel room and took a brief look around, noting the lamp by the door. He turned back to me and adjusted his stance; I saw the bulge of a firearm under his shoulder and mentally thanked myself for not swinging first and asking questions later. Daniels looked directly back at me and reached up to remove his sunglasses. His eyes were brown and distinctly normal looking; no paranormal glow. "Drop the case," he said bluntly.

I frowned, folding my arms in a defiant gesture. "I'm not dropping anything," I replied. "The Secret Service has no jurisdiction over private investigations."

Daniels looked at me. "The Secret Service has jurisdiction over anything that it deems to be a threat to the President's life," he replied. "At the moment, I am taking you to be that threat." He took a step closer to me. "The Secret Service is conducting its own operations regarding the Angeles de la Muerte, all of which is highly classified." Daniels smiled coldly. "Drop the case now, or I will arrange with some good friends of mine at the CIA to have you dropped into the deepest, darkest hole of the worst black site prison we have."

I did not know what to say, and simply nodded. Daniels nodded back in satisfaction and turned to leave. "Good," he said. "We'll be keeping an eye on you, so I suggest that you don't wander far from here until after the Presidential visit." And with that, he replaced his sunglasses and stepped out into the sunlight, closing the door heavily behind him.

I stood there in the doorway of the motel room, completely taken aback by what had just happened. This situation was getting more bizarre with every passing day. "What the hell is going on here?" I wondered aloud.

"Who was that?" Anahita asked.

I jumped and spun on my heels. My guardian angel was perched on the edge of the bed, watching me with a curious expression. She seemed momentarily startled by my sudden movements. "What's wrong?" she asked.

"Nothing," I replied, taking a deep breath and shaking my head a little. "The whole sudden appearance thing that you and your boss do is a little unnerving."

Anahita's eyes flickered with confusion for a few moments, and then widened a little in realisation. "Ah, I see," she said, and then, to my surprise, she smiled a little sheepishly. "My apologies," she said. "We're so used to just teleporting around everywhere that we forget that it can be a little surprising for those who do not."

I shrugged. "Surprising is putting it lightly," I said, leaning against the wall.

Anahita's eyes flicked back to the doorway. "Who was that?" she asked.

"Secret Service," I replied, rubbing the bridge of my nose. I glanced up and, seeing Anahita's confused expression, explained, "They're the specialist protection group for the leader of this country."

"Ah," Anahita nodded; then frowned. "What would they want with you?" she asked.

"I seem to have ruffled some feathers," I remarked, glancing out of the window next to the motel room's door. I watched Daniels approach a blacked-out sedan similar to the one I had seen at the angel's compound, take one last glance towards my room, and then climb in and drive away. "There's something linking the Secret Service to the angels," I mused, watching the sedan disappear down the road. "I'll need to watch my step with them poking their noses in."

"What about watching your step with that woman from last night?" Anahita asked quietly.

I spun on my heel to stare at her. "How do you-?" I began, and then my astonishment turned to anger. "Are you spying on me?" I demanded. "I know you're my guardian and all, but that gives you no right to infringe on my privacy! Can you see everything that happens with me when you're not around?"

Anahita's expression grew a little harder. "I am connected to you emotionally as part of my role to protect you when you feel you are in danger," she said in a clipped tone. "I do not spy on those I protect, but I do unintentionally feel what they are feeling in times of heightened emotion." She emphasised the word 'unintentionally' as if it was a particularly undesirable thing. She paused and glanced down at the bed she was perched on. "There was certainly a lot of heightened emotion in here last night," she remarked.

I snorted, folding my arms. "Not jealous, by any chance?" I remarked.

Anahita looked at me with a level of disgust that was usually reserved for insects discovered in food. "Angels do not find humans to be particularly worthy of such thoughts," she remarked.

I smirked. "Tell that to my ancestor," I replied. I saw something odd flicker across Anahita's face, but she repressed it quickly. I may have touched on a nerve, so instead of pressing further I asked, "What're you doing here?"

Anahita stood up. "Alleam requires you to assist me,"

she said.

I laughed a little. "The last time Alleam asked for my assistance, I almost got slaughtered by a room full of infernal bikers," I observed.

Anahita's expression hardened a little. "That was without my knowledge," she replied. "In this matter, you will be alongside me."

"Doing what exactly?" I asked.

Anahita studied me for a long moment. "Using your skills to gain knowledge on the location of something we need to recover," she finally replied in a weary tone.

"No," I said suddenly, surprised at myself even as I said it.

Anahita blinked, completely dumbfounded. "Excuse me?" she asked.

"I said no," I replied, and I realised that I was angry. I pointed at her accusingly. "I'm tired," I said, my tone rising as I spoke. "I'm tired of being used as a pawn by you and your boss whilst being kept in the dark. I'm tired of being thrown into potentially lethal situations without knowing the full picture of what's going on. And I'm certainly tired of being treated like a potential security threat when I have done nothing but help you people since you approached me."

Anahita glared at me. "You broke into the compound of the angels without instruction," she replied in a low tone, the lack of volume doing little to hide her annoyance at me. "You constantly question mine and Alleam's judgement and you consort with Elioud outsiders like that woman from last night with little regard for the security or seriousness of our cause." She cocked her head a little and added spitefully, "How exactly would you like to be treated?"

"I would like to be treated like a human being!" I shouted back. "I would like to be treated as a person with feelings and worries and not just a mannequin with the ability to see through walls that you can't! I would like to be treated as the valuable individual that you all proclaim me to be in this little game of traitorous insurgency that you are involved in against your own side!"

Anahita moved so fast that I barely registered it. One moment she was sitting on the bed; the next, she had one hand around my throat and had lifted me a few inches from the floor. Her face was twisted in an angry snarl and her eyes were flashing a blinding white-blue that, filling my vision at such a close range, forced me to close my eyes to protect my sight. "I am not a traitor!" she shouted, her voice filling the room like a megaphone. "How dare you of all people call me-"

I am not entirely sure how I did what happened next. As Anahita screamed at me, her grip tightening around my windpipe, my eyes flicked around the room desperately for something to help. My gaze fell upon the bedside table standing only a few feet away. Something in my mind went back to what Gemma had said to me the previous night; "…you just sort of focus on what you want to happen in your mind's eye and let it happen…"

And that is what I did.

The table lifted from the floor and flew across the short space between us almost too fast for me to comprehend. The heavy wooden furniture slammed into the side of Anahita and clipped her head, causing her to lose her grip and stumble sideways. I fell to the floor where she had been holding me and gasped for air, my hands cradling the painful bruises I could feel rising around my throat. I rolled onto my back and scrabbled backwards as far as I could against the far wall, my heart pounding with adrenaline as I watched Anahita.

Anahita was on her knees, one hand cradling the back of her head where the furniture had hit her. She turned to look back at me; her expression looked pained, but not physically.

If anything, she seemed frightened. For a moment I thought she was going to launch herself at me again and I tensed, but instead she slowly climbed to her feet and stood there, looking down at me with a combination of wariness and anger. "Very well," she said. "If it makes you feel any better to know; we're going to recover a weapon."

I took a few deep breaths, my breathing becoming easier with every moment. "What kind of weapon?" I asked after a moment, pulling myself back to my feet and balancing against the wall whilst I waited for my head to stop spinning.

Anahita eyed me carefully. "A missing weapon," she replied. "A weapon that does not belong in the hands of those who currently hold it, and a weapon we need to obtain in order to stop the Horseman when he is revealed."

I frowned at her, my thoughts becoming less jumbled as my head stopped spinning. "Why haven't you gone after this weapon already?" I asked.

"We did not know the location," Anahita answered, absently rubbing the back of her head again. She appeared to have no physical injury, which I found both fascinating and rather disturbing. "That was what we needed Furcas for, to get the general location of the weapon," she added.

"So what do you need me for?" I asked.

Anahita smiled. "To pinpoint it," she replied.

Chapter 12

We were standing on a ledge overlooking a quarry. I only took a moment to get my balance back, getting used to this manner of moving around via teleportation. We both crouched low and made our way to the edge, looking down over the vast expanse of excavation below us.

The quarry was a flurry of activity. Trucks moved constantly, flowing in and out of the main entrance gate further down the perimeter fence. Hundreds of people scurried like armies of ants around the larger vehicles, whilst the sound of digging machinery could be heard from multiple locations. From what I could see, there were several active areas of digging across the entire site. I had packed a few things into a rucksack before we left the motel and now pulled out a pair of binoculars, training them down on the people working. I saw a large number of bikers walking around. "Infernal bikers," I confirmed, glancing over at Anahita. "So the weapon is in one of the areas they are digging?"

Anahita nodded. "That is correct," she confirmed, her eyes surveying the scene below us. "I need to know which area." She turned to look at me. "Can you find out?"

I sighed, looking across the few buildings that littered the floor of the quarry. "Maybe," I hedged, seeking for something that looked worthwhile. "If I can find where the main office is, maybe I can-" and then I broke off with a curse.

Anahita frowned at me. "What?" she asked.

I did not answer, merely pointing in the direction I was looking. Two people in biker jackets were walking across the quarry towards the largest of the temporary buildings. One of them was Astartoth, his sneering expression all-too-familiar from the compound meeting. The other was a woman, and I recognised her as one of the police officers that had attacked me on the first day that I had gone to meet Miriam. Anahita surveyed them both silently as they entered one of the buildings and closed the door behind them. I looked over at her. "That's the one," I muttered.

Anahita nodded. "I would believe so," she agreed.

I took a deep breath and closed my eyes, picturing the building in my mind as if holding a photo. I imagined moving towards it, floating down over the ledge and across the expanse of the quarry. The feeling of lifting from my body started a few moments later and I could suddenly see everything as if I still had my eyes open. I was indeed rushing down across the expanse into the quarry, darting around obstacles and excavation machinery towards the office where Astartoth and the woman had entered. Suddenly I was at the door of the trailer and, with a strange sensation like moving through treacle, I stepped through the wall and into the room.

Astartoth and the woman were standing in the middle of the trailer. The decoration of the office was largely standard; filing cabinets along one wall and a large desk at one end with a map above it depicting the quarry. Unusually, the windows were all shuttered and the only light was from dozens of candles set around the trailer. On the desk, between the two largest candles, a wooden bowl and knife sat in the middle of a small pentacle drawn in melted candle wax. The two stood solemnly facing each-other. I held my breath, fearful of being heard despite not physically being in the room. Astartoth was speaking as I entered. "...to be careful," he was saying. "But above all, we have to move quickly. I have grave fears that we have been discovered in our plot."

The woman frowned in concern. "Beelzebub has discovered us, you think?" she asked.

Astartoth shrugged. "Possibly," he said. "Or perhaps another faction, I don't know for sure. All I know is that Furcas has been missing for almost two days now, and he was the only other within the Earth-based Hell contingent that knew of what we were doing here." He turned to the knife and bowl on the table and picked them up. "We must presume we have been discovered and make haste," he said, turning to the woman.

The woman smiled, straightening her stance as if standing at attention. "I am ready," she said.

Astartoth smiled. He walked across to the woman and faced her, lifting the dagger and the bowl before him. "You have been my loyal servant for a long time, Innana," he said, looking the woman in the eye. "You have been dedicated, faithful and dogged in obeying my commands. Now it is time to take the final step." As he spoke, he handed Innana the bowl and lifted one of his arms so that his hand was over the bowl, palm down. With one deft movement, he swiped the blade across the downturned wrist. There was an audible hiss, and steaming, dark red blood began flowing from Astartoth's veins and into the bowl. Once it was filled, he lowered his wrist, blood still dripping onto the floor, and nodded to Innana. "I give my force to you," he said. "I give my strength and my blessing."

Innana bowed her head solemnly in return. "I give my loyalty to you," she said. "I give my fealty and my subservience." And with that, she lifted the bowl to her lips and drank down the blood greedily. I felt a perceptible change in the room, as if the air was suddenly charged with electricity. A faint humming, off-key and rather unpleasant, sounded at the edge of my hearing. The noise grew to a crescendo that made me reach for my ears in reflex, until Innana lowered the bowl and the noise faded as abruptly as it had begun.

Astartoth smiled. "In preparation for your joining with the Ophanim," he said, "I hereby promote you to the Infernal Choir of Thrones. Satan be praised."

"Satan be praised," Innana replied, grinning broadly with

blood-reddened lips.

I felt my presence weakening and realised that I was pushing my limits for viewing. Quickly, I stole as much information visually from the digging chart on the wall before I suddenly felt myself rushing backwards, up and out of the office and the quarry at an incredible speed until I lurched back into my body and only just managed to prevent myself from crying out in surprise and pain.

Anahita was looking at me anxiously. "What can you tell me?" she asked.

I took a couple of gasps for breath. "Astartoth and Innana are in there," I gasped. "They just went through some sort of promotion ceremony to join Innana to something called an Ophanim." Anahita's face grew ashen, and I frowned at her. "That's what we're here to recover, isn't it?" I asked.

Anahita nodded. "The Ophanim is like a massive battery for the powers of an angel," she replied quietly, glancing down at the quarry. "It accentuates our powers far beyond our normal capabilities."

I raised my eyebrows. "You're pretty strong already," I remarked. "What kind of boost are we talking about here?"

"You ever hear of Sodom and Gomorrah?" Anahita replied.

I caught my breath. "They're about to strap a power source capable of levelling a city to a fallen angel?" I asked.

"Unless we get to it first," Anahita replied grimly. "But we still have time. Innana needs to undergo a ritualised binding process in order for the Ophanim to recognise her as an appropriately ranked angelic entity to utilise its powers." Then Anahita smiled, although I detected a hint of sadness in her expression. "Fortunately, I have held that rank for centuries," she remarked. "I do not need the ritual to join with the Ophanim." She peered down into the quarry again. "Do you know which dig site it is?" she asked.

I nodded, pointing towards the far end of the quarry. "There," I said, referring to one large entrance into a series of mining tunnels. As I spoke, a horn sounded. People began to pile out of the various dig sites and into the main area of the quarry. "Shift change," I remarked.

Anahita nodded. "Then we have to go now," she replied, standing up.

"What?" I said, looking up at her. "Aren't we going to pull in some backup?"

"No time," Anahita replied. "If Innana has been promoted, it means the joining ceremony is imminent. Plus this shift change will mean that there will be a minimum number of people in the tunnels right now." She looked down at me. "I need you to get into those tunnels and secure the Ophanim for me," she said.

"You're insane," I snapped back, standing up next to her. "You expect me to secure the heavenly equivalent of an atomic bomb on my own?"

"Not on your own," Anahita replied tersely. "I will be causing a distraction and getting the fallen angels as far away from you as possible." She looked back down at the quarry. "This is an illegal operation according to the treaties between Heaven and Hell," she remarked. "As soon as I start throwing angelic energies around down there, the Heavenly faction will notice." She looked back at me again. "There will be a ritual circle set up around the Ophanim as part of the joining ceremony; I need you to break that circle. It will stop the ritual being able to take place immediately. Then we hold out until the Heavenly side are close to arriving and the Hellish forces start trying to escape, and slip the Ophanim out."

I shook my head in bewilderment. "This is insane," I repeated.

"This is necessary," Anahita replied. "Are you ready?"

I looked back down at the quarry, at the hundreds of

bikers and workers teeming in and out of the site. "As I will ever be," I replied.

"Good," Anahita replied. "Now, hold on tight."

※

We were flying.

Anahita had scooped me up and launched us both off the edge of the quarry before I could react. I reached one hand up and shielded my eyes as we charged down towards the quarry floor in a straight line, the ground rushing towards us at an alarming rate. We were only a few feet from the floor before we suddenly turned, flying across the quarry and hugging the ground like a fighter jet, dodging between buildings and people at blindingly fast speeds. Several shouts of alarm rang out as people noticed us, and I heard a siren begin sounding somewhere.

"Get ready," Anahita shouted, and I braced myself. We tore straight across the quarry towards the mine shafts at the far end, the people thinning out now as we moved away from the main body of people that were still in confusion. As we approached the entrance, I saw a number of security guards rushing forward, all aiming automatic weapons at us. I flinched in anticipation, but Anahita stretched one arm out in front of us and began firing bolts of blue energy in their direction. Three guards were hit and simply faded away in a flash of white light. The others began scrambling in various directions, firing haphazardly in our direction as they went.

We came to rest outside the entrance of the mine shaft. Anahita dropped me onto my feet and I rushed across to one of the guns dropped by the fleeing guards. I checked the magazine and nodded to Anahita. "I'll make my way inside," I said. "You watch my back until the cavalry starts arriving."

Anahita nodded, and was about to reply when we head

a screeching noise. I turned and saw two flashes of red light charging in our direction. Astartoth and Innana had heard us and were moving to intercept us at the head of a much larger army of workers and bikers. Anahita turned to me with a grim expression. "Go," she said. "I'll hold them off." And before I could say another word, she had disappeared again into the sky.

I waited no longer, and I turned my back on the scene and ran down into the mine shaft as fast as I dared over the uneven floor. The natural light began to fade rather quickly, and soon I was simply bathed in the artificial yellow glow of the lights hanging from the ceiling. The tunnels began to curve and branch off and I paused, wondering where to go next. The sounds of battle were reaching me faintly from the tunnel entrance. I had no idea how long Anahita needed to hold off the fallen angels and their allies until the Heavenly faction turned up to ruin their day. I forced myself to calm down and closed my eyes, reaching my senses outwards along the paths ahead. I felt myself flowing along the tunnel ways, seeing the routes ahead of me as if they were clear as day through my Second Sight, until my senses touched something powerful and I recoiled in surprise. I had mentally brushed against something massive and slumbering, as if I had stumbled across a sleeping bear. "The Ophanim," I muttered. I opened my eyes and turned down the path that I needed.

It was half-buried in the ground at the centre of a large excavation. Black candles and backwards-written scrawls covered the floor, with a trail of bones marking a circle around the place where it sat. Crystals were set at equidistant points around the circle, letting out a slight hum of energy. The Ophanim itself was about the size of a small family car. It consisted of a set of interlocked rings at ninety-degree angles from each-other, giving the impression of a spherical frame with no coverings. It appeared to be made of stone, with ornate carvings along each ring that I did not even begin to understand. I stood in its wake for a moment, simply looking at it with awe.

I heard shrieking again and jumped. I turned, looking back up the tunnel. Closing my eyes, I hastily extended my Sight. I saw Innana blazing down towards me, her face twisted in fury, her eyes flashing crimson red. She must have gotten past Anahita and was now charging down towards the Ophanim, determined to claim her prize. I had to think fast. I ran across to the circle surrounding the Ophanim and, with one heavy stamp, crushed one of the crystals into dust. The hum in the air faded as the circle was broken, and I heard Innana cry out again in rage, as if she had somehow sensed it. I looked around frantically, searching for another exit to the cavern I found myself in. There was another tunnel behind the Ophanim and I ran around the weapon and down it as fast as I could.

"How *dare* you!" I heard Innana roaring out from somewhere behind me. "I have been preparing for this moment since before you were born." Her voice became momentarily louder as she entered the chamber containing the Ophanim and pursued me up the next tunnel. "Decades of earning my place, proving my loyalty," she continued, ranting in a hysterical fashion. Still running, I ducked down a side tunnel and tried to slow my breathing as much as I could, hoping that I could somehow evade her in these catacombs below the quarry. I suddenly had a flash of nausea and, on instinct, threw myself to one side. Innana came crashing through the stone wall a split second later, mere inches from where I had been standing. She turned towards me and howled in anger as I scrabbled to my feet and continued to run, ducking down yet another passageway before she could potentially hit me with any kind of supernatural projectile. It was only moments later that I realised, with panic, that I had entered a dead end.

"You fool," I heard Innana sneer behind me, and I spun around to face her. She was standing at the end of the short corridor of rock, the aura around her body ablaze with amber and red light. She bared her teeth at me and I saw that she had far too many, just as with Astartoth. "You may have set back our plans, but they are not irreplaceable." She raised a hand out in front of her and I saw a red light begin to glow in her hand, gradually building with size and luminosity. "And now you will pay with your life," she declared.

I closed my eyes as the red glare from the energy in her hand began to illuminate the cavern as if with daylight. I heard Innana roar and I flinched in expectation. When nothing happened, I opened my eyes again.

Innana was on her back. The source of the light had changed; no longer was it the blazing aura of the fallen angel, but the blue-white piercing energy of Anahita. She stood in the entrance, towering over Innana, looking down at her Hellish counterpart with a cool gaze. Her eyes were glowing with an energy I had not seen in her before, and on her forehead I could see a glowing symbol; the shape of the Ophanim, its interlocked wheels visibly turning within the tattoo. Anahita looked down at Innana for a long moment. "The Heavenly forces will be here shortly," she then said quietly. "I suggest you make your exit before they arrive."

Innana scowled up at Anahita. "You *stole it*," she hissed. "You stole my rightful powers."

I saw Anahita's eyes flash. "They were stolen to begin with," she replied in a hard tone. "I am just making sure they do not fall into the wrong hands."

Innana laughed; that made Anahita blink in confusion. "You think you're so high and mighty?" the fallen angel sneered, looking Anahita up and down with derision. "You're as lost as I am. You just don't know it yet."

Anahita just levelled a gaze at Innana. "Disappear or

meet your maker," she replied calmly. "I would not recommend the second option."

Innana stared daggers back at Anahita, and spat upon the floor. Her spittle hissed and visibly burned into the rock. Then, with a clap of energy that echoed like thunder, she simply vanished.

Anahita watched the ground where Innana had lain for a few moments, as if checking that she was definitely gone. Then she turned to look at me. "Are you okay?" she asked. Her eyes were still blazing with blue-white light and the tattoo-like imprint of the Ophanim on her head pulsed and moved in an unreal and disconcerting way.

I nodded my head. "Nothing a bottle of whisky won't solve," I replied with forced light heartedness. Then I asked, cautiously, "How about you?"

Anahita smiled slowly, dreamily. "The best I have felt in years," she replied.

I nodded dubiously. "Uh huh," I replied. "How do we get that massive hunk of rock out of here then?" I nodded back down the passageway towards the cavern with the Ophanim.

"What?" Anahita asked, an expression of confusion on her face. Then she smiled. "Oh, I understand," she said. "That stone depiction of the Ophanim was merely a storage device for the energy." She reached her hand up to lightly touch the depiction on her forehead. "The energy is within me now," she replied.

"That's a lot of power to be carrying around," I remarked.

I looked cautious. Anahita noticed and smiled at me. "Do not worry, Sam," she said, a genuine trace of happiness within her tone. "We are one step closer to the end." And then she beckoned me closer. "Let us now take the next step."

And, in a flash of light, I felt us teleporting away.

Chapter 13

I was standing in a garden.

Anahita had dropped me off at the motel after teleporting us back from the quarry. She had seemed unfocused and dreamlike, as if completely overwhelmed with euphoria. The Ophanim tattoo on her forehead continued to glow ominously and I elected to make no comment. She had vanished shortly after leaving me outside my room, telling me that she had to report in to Alleam. I had turned to my motel room door, opened it and stepped through to find myself in a garden.

I turned to find that the doorway had disappeared entirely. Fields of green stretched in all directions, disappearing into the vanishing point. A sun blazed down on me from overhead, the light and heat intense but not overpowering. It was a relaxed, pleasant place and I found myself instinctively relaxing, a wave of peace washing over my mind. I had no idea where I was, but I liked it.

"I said that we would meet again," a voice said.

I turned. Norman had appeared from nowhere. He was smiling at me with that gentle expression of his, the long, blonde hair around his shoulders waving gently in an unfelt breeze. He wore loose-fitting white robes. He took a few paces closer and embraced me. I did not move, felt no discomfort or surprise; merely peace. He released me and smiled again. "I apologise for pulling you away from the place you expected to be," he said. "This is the only place that we are able to talk without being heard."

I glanced around at the greenery. "And where exactly is that?" I asked.

"In your head," Norman replied, then shrugged. "And also in another place. It's hard to describe using your current conception of reality." He then turned and gazed across the landscape, across the gentle plains and grasslands. "We are where it all began," he replied. "Where humanity was first thrown from."

I looked around, trying to understand what Norman was saying. Then I caught my breath as I realised. "Eden," I breathed.

Norman turned back to me and nodded gently. "Yes," he said solemnly. "The Garden of Eden. Half-way between your terrestrial world and the realms of Heaven, the Garden connects both." He sighed, looking back across the fields at some distant, unseen object. "Now it is empty," he said, and I detected a twinge of bitterness in his voice. "Left to quietly fade, with nobody allowed to repopulate; a monument, they claim, to what humanity gave up in order to have free will." Norman turned to look back at me. "You know that nobody dies here?" he asked. "There's no pain, no disease, no distress." He shook his head despairingly. "Such a waste," he muttered.

I looked around, awed by the significance of where we stood. "Are we really here?" I asked in a hushed whisper.

Norman thought for a moment before responding. "Part of us is," he replied. "The Garden does not quite exist in your world as you may readily understand it."

"So this is some sort of telepathy?" I asked, turning back to Norman. He merely smiled, not answering. I sighed. "So what do you want?" I asked.

Norman shook his head. "No, my friend," he replied. "The question is; what do you want to ask me?"

I looked at him for a long moment. "Ophanims," I said. "What are they?"

Norman's brow creased a little. "Ah," he said. "The first has been found?" When I nodded in affirmation, he sighed. "Ophanims are weapons," he replied. "They are a source of power derived from the Holy Throne of Heaven itself." He set his mouth in a grim line. "They are terrible weapons, only unleashed in the most extreme of circumstances."

"Holy nukes," I muttered to myself. Then I frowned. "You said the first one has been found," I recalled. "There are more?"

Norman nodded. "Three in total," he replied.

I raised my brow. "So Heaven has three holy equivalents of nuclear warheads missing from their weapons inventory?" I asked disbelievingly. "How does that happen?"

"They were stolen," Norman replied. "During the First Fall, when I and many others left Heaven."

"You stole them?" I asked.

Norman shook his head. "No, but our leader did," he replied. "The angel we followed into our exile. He felt it would provide us insurance against Heaven trying to capture us in the future." Norman's eyes grew distant for a moment as he recalled. "We didn't expect Heaven would try to wipe us out with The Flood," he said quietly. "The angel of the Waters, Yardna; one of the most powerful of her choir, was commanded to unleash several Ophanims upon the oceans, multiplying the waters until all was covered and drowned. Those of us who tried to escape to the skies and the other dimensions were hunted by the Holy Throne's armies. Only a few of us slipped through the net." Norman sighed, and for the first time since I had met him I thought he looked tired. "We have been hunted constantly ever since," he finished.

"And you lost the weapons in the process," I concluded.

Norman nodded. "The only person who knew their locations for sure was our leader," he replied.

"And Alleam needs them to take down the Horsemen," I mused to myself. Then I asked, "So is this leader of yours still around? Surely we could just track him down and find out the other locations."

Norman smiled sadly. "I'm afraid it isn't that easy," he replied softly.

I snorted. "Yeah, it never is," I muttered, looking away and across the rolling fields.

I was a little surprised when I felt a hand on my shoulder. Norman had stepped closer to me again and was looking at me with a hugely sympathetic look on his face. "I would love to tell you more, Sam," he said quietly. "I hate prolonging the frustration and the pain you must be feeling." Norman's hand slipped from my shoulder and he studied me for a moment. "We are dealing with massive forces of power and knowledge the likes of which have not been seen on Earth in centuries," he continued. "The sheer scale of what is to come would destroy your sanity if it is not introduced with a gradual acceptance of what you are capable of and the correct mindset with which to receive it." He smiled at me. "As annoying as this must be, we're doing it for your own good," he finished.

I studied Norman for a long moment. I wanted to be angry at him for keeping me in the dark, much like all the other angelic beings I had met so far. But the sorrow in his crystal blue eyes made those feelings dissipate. He genuinely was sorry that he could not say more. So I merely nodded and asked, "Is there anything useful you can tell me about the Horseman I'm supposed to be tracking?"

Norman thought for a moment. "He is the Horseman of Conquest," he replied. "The first to ride out in the Book of Revelation; He turns people's minds with images of glory and twists the most horrendous desires in humanity to carry out his wishes in preparation for damning the sinful to Hell." He studied me for a long moment. "Remember this, Sam," he said. "Remember what he can twist you to be; what they all can twist you to be."

There was a faint, piercing ringing in my ears, and I

glanced around a little in confusion. "So what should I do now?" I asked.

Norman smiled. "Keep doing what you're doing," he said. "Keep trying to do the best you can, and remember the path you want to tread."

The ringing was getting louder now, boring into my head with greater volume every second. I put my hands over my ears, but it did nothing to help. "What is that?" I shouted over the din.

Norman smiled. "The next chapter, Sam," he replied.

I blinked, and suddenly I was back in the motel, standing in the doorway to my room as if I had just walked in. The deafening ringing noise was the telephone, shrieking its desire to be answered. I blinked a couple of times as I regained my bearings. Then I hastened across the room to the telephone and picked it up. "Hello?" I asked warily.

"It's me," Miriam replied, her tone hushed and hurried. "10pm, two miles south of the angel's Compound."

I leaned into the receiver, my heart pounding with sudden anxiety. "What's going on?" I demanded.

Miriam's voice was sombre. "The Horseman is riding in," she replied.

Chapter 14

I squinted at the headlights of the van as Miriam pulled up on the side of the road and killed the engine. We were a couple of miles south of the angel's Compound; I had left a rental car parked not far off the main road in case I had to escape this way. I had travelled light, not wanting to be carrying anything bulky that could make things difficult getting into the compound. I had chanced a quick visit back to my office and, finding nobody watching it at that moment, hastily retrieved my handgun and some spare ammunition. I had no idea how a gun would work against angelic beings, but I certainly wanted to have the option available to try. I was only waiting a few minutes in the dark, listening intently to the noises in the fields, when Miriam arrived. She was driving towards the compound from the city, and from the low level of the chassis on the van I presumed it was laden with supplies. As the engine went silent, she climbed down from the cab and walked across to me, her face filled with solemnity and worry. "Are you ready?" she asked.

I nodded. "As I'll ever be," I replied. "So what does this entail?"

Miriam beckoned me. "Follow me," she said, and led me to the back of the van. She pulled open the rear doors to reveal piles of rectangular crates inside. She pulled one of them open and reached in, pulling out a candle and a jar of clear, viscous liquid. I could see in the glow of the van's internal light that the jar's label read 'Holy Oil.' Miriam unscrewed the lid and turned to me. "Sit down on the tail bar," she requested. I complied. Miriam dipped the first two fingers of her free hand into the oil and proceeded to mark a cross on my forehead. "Benedictus es," she began, reciting in Latin. "Domine Deus noster, rex totius orbis..." As Miriam continued the Latin, she reached into her pocket and pulled a lighter free, using it to light the candle. She waved it over me in the motion of a cross and then, holding it above me, tilted the candle and let some of the wax splash down onto my forehead.

As soon as the warm, clay-like wax hit my skin, I felt a sudden wave of dizziness and swayed. My vision began to blur, everything beginning to go dark. I heard Miriam calling my name, faintly as if she was suddenly a long way away. But I was not listening. I was staring at something in front of me. In the middle of the darkness, almost blinding in its light, were a pair of interlocked wheels spinning slowly around each other. The wheels were covered in deep blue, piercing eyes, each one of which stared at me accusingly as it passed by in rotation. It was an Ophanim.

And it was angry at me.

The image faded and I found myself leaning against the side of the van in the evening darkness, a concerned Miriam shaking my shoulders. "Are you okay?" she asked urgently, her eyes full of worry.

I nodded, feeling a little groggy. "Yeah," I said, waving her away. "I don't know what happened there, but…" I trailed off for a moment, and then shook my head. "Is it done?" I asked her.

She nodded. "The sanctification is complete," she replied. "You will be able to pass into the compound undetected by angelic security procedures." She nodded to one of the crates. "That one is empty. You'll need to climb inside and be as quiet as possible."

I nodded. After a few moments I was secured inside the crate, and Miriam closed the lid. I heard a grating of wood from outside and realised that she must have placed another crate on top of mine to minimise the possibility of somebody searching it. I felt a sudden rush of claustrophobia and forced myself to calm down; if those angels found me because I freaked out on the way in, I was as good as dead. I heard Miriam climb back into the cab and restart the engine, moving the van off down the road.

I rode in darkness for what seemed like ages, although it must have only been around ten minutes given how close we were to the compound. I felt Miriam slow the van to a halt and exchange muffled words with somebody. We must have been at the main gate. I heard a clicking noise and the van's engine suddenly got louder; somebody had opened the rear doors of the van. I held my breath, fighting the instinctual urge to escape from the enclosed space I was in. A few tense moments passed, I heard somebody shout something that I did not quite hear, and then the van doors closed again. I breathed a huge sigh of relief as I felt the vehicle move forward again. I was in. I felt the vehicle turn a couple of times and then come to a halt before the engine died again. I was left in darkened silence, waiting for whatever happened next.

A few moments later, I heard a scraping noise above me. Dull light suddenly poured into the crate as the lid was lifted and I blinked a few times to get my vision clear. Miriam was standing over me, looking around furtively. I sat up in the crate and looked around. The back doors to the van were open and I could see that we were parked up inside one of the compound garages, the roller door slid shut. I could hear a cacophony of engines and voices shouting from beyond as the angels organised themselves for the visit of the Horseman. "Hurry," Miriam whispered, pulling me by the arm out of the crate. "There will be security sweeps through here soon. You need to get across to the next building along and hide yourself away; nobody will be in there."

"What if they look for me?" I asked, climbing down from the van.

She shook her head. "Unlikely," she replied. "They will

have roving patrols, but they will be specifically looking for anything they can detect as non-sanctified." She closed the van doors as quietly as she could and looked back to me. "I have to get into position myself," she whispered. "You need to move now!"

I nodded. "Thank you," I said quietly, then turned and sprinted across the garage to one of the side doors. Gently, I opened the door a couple of inches and peered through the crack. There was a short alleyway between the garage and the next building along that Miriam had indicated. There was nobody in sight. As quickly and as quietly as I could, I slipped out of the doorway and crept across the open space to the next side door, praying desperately that nobody would see me. I slid through the door and into the next building just as I heard voices behind me in the alley. I quietly closed the door and pressed myself against the wall, holding my breath until I was sure the voices had passed by. Then I looked around.

I was in an office, the gloom picking out the outlines of desks and chairs. A set of doors led off one wall into various closets and storage areas. I opened the closest door gently, found that there was plenty of space to hide myself and climbed inside. The darkness enveloped me again as I closed the door and pressed myself against the back wall, focusing on controlling my heart rate and my breathing. I was going to need all of my concentration to pull this off and I needed to have as level a head as I could. I was close to having all this over and done with; I just needed to hold it together for a little while longer. I closed my eyes and began to focus.

The feeling of movement came even quicker this time; all the recent practice at using my supernatural talents was definitely paying off. I felt my mind moving forwards, out through the closed cupboard door and across the office, gliding as smoothly and elegantly as I imagined a ghost would. I passed through the outer office walls with only a faint trace of discomfort and found myself standing in the courtyard, watching the cacophony of noise and activity.

The courtyard was organised chaos; bikes were moving around, parking up neatly in rows at the edge of the compound walls. The central space of the courtyard had been cleared and a small podium erected, from which somebody could address a crowd. The Horseman, I presumed. I saw Banniel standing at the centre of it all, talking to several bikers and a couple of people in dark suits. They looked out of place in comparison to the rest of the leather and denim-clad bikers, so I moved towards them.

"...sure that everything is prepared?" I heard one of the suited men ask Banniel. As I got closer, I caught my breath in surprise. It was Daniels, the Secret Service agent who had turned up at my motel door a few days before. He was wearing the same clothes I had seen him in before, and his face showed signs of tiredness and strain. At least I was not the only one missing a few nights' sleep, I thought.

I saw Banniel nod. "Everything is in order," he replied. "We have been undertaking security sweeps throughout the day; nothing out of the ordinary. We are completely secure."

I suppressed a victorious grin; Miriam's sanctification ritual was obviously working. I only had to hope that the security would not look too carefully in areas that they had already passed through until I had the information I needed. It was a risk, but I had to take it.

After a few more moments of activity, the bikers were assembled. They stood in sombre ranks with Banniel at the front and centre; I presumed it was in some kind of rank order, as I saw Miriam and the other human helpers standing at the back of the crowd. I saw Banniel turn and nod to Daniels, who reached into his pocket and pulled out a radio transmitter. He muttered a few words into it and then I saw the front gates of the compound begin to open with a groan of metal.

A large, black sedan pulled into the centre of the compound. Daniels hurried across to the rear door and pulled it open. I heard a voice from inside say, "Well, thank-you Daniels, much obliged," in a slow, relaxed Southern drawl. The passenger stepped out and I gasped.

Francis Bowman, the Vice President of the United States, squinted out across the brightly lit compound at the crowd. His grandfatherly smile still looked as gentle as it had on the television interview, and yet now the gentle-looking old man gave me chills. He was wearing an expensive-looking charcoal grey suit and his hair was slicked back neatly, as if he was meeting supporters on a campaign trail junket. He shook Banniel's hand briefly and exchanged a few warm words that I did not quite hear before climbing the podium to survey the assembled angels and their human associates. The courtyard was dead silent, the only noises being the hum of the floodlights in each corner of the courtyard and the gentle rush of wind through the trees. Agent Daniels stood next to Bowman at the edge of the podium, eyeing the crowd as if every person there was as security threat. Bowman leaned across to Daniels and muttered a few low words. Daniel's eyes moved over the crowd slowly, briefly passing over my extra-bodily location in doing so, and nodded once. Bowman stood back up and surveyed the crowd. Nobody spoke. Everyone waited.

Eventually Bowman smiled. "My friends," he said. "We have come a long way." He paused for a moment, his eyes locking onto each person in the crowd. For a moment I thought he was looking directly at me and my heart leapt in my throat, but then his eyes moved on a moment later without any indication of concern. "We have endured many hardships," he continued. "We have been forced to withdraw from this world as the faith of humanity waned, distracted as they were by the rational liberalism of this age and the temptations of modern society put forward by our adversaries from the forces of Satan." There was a brief murmur of agreement from the crowd and Bowman smiled. "No longer," he declared quietly, placing both hands firmly on the podium. "No longer do we allow humanity to have its own way. No longer do we let them continue to forget where they came from and to whom they owe their existence." There was another wave of agreement, this time louder. Bowman looked across at Banniel. "Under the guidance of your eminent leader," he continued, "we are now in a position to begin enacting our final plans to bring about God's Kingdom upon Earth." Another wave of agreements from the crowd, interspersed with a few cheers. I could feel the crowd getting worked up as Bowman spoke, as if there was an electric vibe in the air that was antagonising their mood. I realised at that moment that it was affecting me too; I had taken a few 'steps' forward from where my mind stood, edging closer to the podium. My heart was racing and I realised my fists were clenched. My mind was shouting at me from a rational corner of my brain not to be so transfixed on the politician and that something had changed in my surroundings, but I was having a hard time focusing on anything else but Bowman's face.

"We will bring the righteous back to their rightful place on this world," Bowman declared, his voice louder than before. The grandfatherly demeanour had seamlessly changed into something more domineering and charismatic, like a General on the eve of a great battle. "We will ensure the sinful take their rightful place alongside Lucifer in Hell. We will break open the Seven Seals and unleash His wrath upon the sinners of this world that has not been seen since the first days that humanity was cast from God's warmth and kindness in the Garden of Eden." Bowman looked around the angels, his eyes shining with a fanatical fervour. "And the world will remember that it started here," he declared. "Heaven will remember you all as heroes, bringing forth the light of God and casting aside the sinful like in the days of Sodom and Gomorrah." There was a loud cheer from the crowd and I found myself urged to join in. I forced myself not to shout aloud; I may not have actually physically been in the courtyard to be heard, but I did not know if security was nearby my physical hiding place and did not want to risk the possibility of shouting out and being overheard. It was then that I realised the change in my surroundings that my rationality had been trying to warn me about; Agent Daniels had disappeared from the edge of the podium.

Bowman let the crowd cheer for a while and then raised his hands for silence. "We have to be careful in these last few days," he replied. "We have to make sure that our plans are foolproof and that our security is paramount. We must expunge those within our ranks who may feel that their faith is wavering, or who may work against us completely."

And then he looked directly at me.

"We have intruders amongst us right now," he said quietly.

My heart skipped a beat.

Agent Daniels came crashing through the door of the office cupboard before I could react.

Chapter 15

The first slap brought me around.

I cried out in pain, the side of my face searing hot with electric tingling along my nerve endings. I tried to curl myself into a ball and realised that I could not move any of my limbs. After a moment the pain began to subside and I opened my eyes.

I was tied to a chair, inside one of the bike garages, the centre of which had been cleared out for my presence. There were several floodlights shining on me from different angles, only allowing me to see a short distance in any direction before the glare changed everything to darkness. I could still hear the noise of people beyond the garage walls; obviously whatever preparations Bowman had come here to finalise were still being undertaken.

"Welcome back," a voice addressed me. I squinted as Banniel stepped out of the gloom, his face illuminated briefly by the floodlights before he became little more than an outline. He stood in front of me, his arms crossed. "We have questions for you," the angel said. Despite the gloom in which his facial features were mostly hidden, I could still see his blue eyes piercing into me. It was unnerving.

I tasted something metallic in my mouth and spat blood to one side. "Would love to help you," I replied. My voice was hoarse and I realised that I was very thirsty. "Unfortunately that would leave me surplus to your requirements," I continued, looking up at Banniel. "And I don't fancy moving on to meet your boss anytime soon."

Banniel swept his hand across his torso in a sudden motion. He was at least twelve feet away, and yet I felt the jolt of pain across my face so hard it forced my head to one side. I cried out in pain. Banniel took a couple of steps closer. "How do you contact Alleam?" he asked.

I took a few deep breaths, trying to ignore the lingering pain in my face. Truthfully, I was terrified; I was sure that Banniel was going lightly on me right now and had no doubt that he could atomise me with a single gesture. I had no idea where Miriam was or how long Alleam would leave things before he tried to check up on our welfare. I thought about calling in Anahita but decided against it; she may end up being outnumbered and destroyed, presuming she could even get here.

"She couldn't, I'm afraid," a drawling voice affirmed. I looked up to see Bowman step forward to stand next to Banniel. He was gently smiling, the fingers of one hand tapping against his thigh in a habitual fashion. Reading the look on my face, he nodded. "That's right," he said softly. "I'm able to read your surface thoughts, much like a certain mutual friend of ours. That's how I detected where you were hiding." He cocked his head at me, eyes boring intently into my own. "Norman; that's what he's calling himself now, is it?" He smirked. "Well, as soon as we locate Alleam, I'm sure I will have to catch up on old times with Norman once we find his location."

"How do you contact Alleam?" Banniel asked again, his tone harsher.

I flinched a little in expectation of another strike of energy, but nothing came. I shook my head. "He contacts me," I replied, my words slurred a little by a growing bruise I could feel in the side of my face. "In person; no other way."

"You're lying," Bowman replied smoothly, folding his arms. "Don't try and talk your way around me, boy; I know exactly how you got in here, using that fool girl Sister Miriam to sanctify you against our normal methods of detection." He smiled cruelly.

I panicked a little, realising that there was no escape

from this man. My thoughts immediately flooded with concern for Miriam, wondering what they had done to her. I forced my mind to go blank, desperately trying not to think of anything to do with Alleam. Bowman stared at me intently for a few moments. "You can block your mind with blandness and darkness for as long as you like," he remarked. "But I can get hold of information like that just by touching you. I'm sure you've seen Norman's gifts at work." He leaned forward towards me, his blue eyes glittering menacingly. "Trust me when I say you don't want to feel what that's like from me."

"We're wasting time," Banniel growled. He looked across at Bowman. "Just rip the information out of his brain and be done with it."

Bowman barely acknowledged Banniel with a glance. "Always to the quick punch, my dear friend," he replied softly, keeping his eyes on me. "This man has a valuable gift; we should offer him salvation before we provide damnation." Then he took another step towards me. "Leave us alone awhile," he ordered.

Banniel looked dubious, his eyes shifting suspiciously between myself and the Vice President. "Are you sure?"

Bowman turned. I did not see the look on his face, but Banniel's expression changed rather quickly to one of grim but hasty acknowledgement. He turned on his heel and walked out of the garage, closing the door behind him with an echo that lingered for a few seconds. Bowman and I were alone and for a few moments, nobody spoke. Then he smiled, reached out and put his hand on my shoulder. I flinched, expecting some sort of pain to ensure, but nothing happened. Bowman squeezed my shoulder gently. "Son," he said softly. "You have been sincerely misinformed about my role here on your planet."

I looked up at him warily. "So far as I understand," I replied, "You're the first in a wave of angels that will bring about the end of the world as I know it."

Bowman tilted his head a little in acknowledgement. "A fair assessment," he replied. "But why is that such a bad thing?"

"Because millions of innocent people will die," I replied.

Bowman laughed. His cackle echoed around the cavernous garage, disappearing into the gloom beyond the spotlights only to return from somewhere behind me. "My dear boy," he said, his voice filled with mirth. "Nobody is innocent. Mankind has been guilty of sin since Eve decided she had an urge for fruit." Bowman walked around me, slipping out of my eyesight in a very unnerving way. "That's what Jesus died for," he said from somewhere behind me. "He took on the sins of your species to bring you back to God. But that only works when people accept Jesus as their saviour." He reappeared on my other side, watching me closely. "The majority of your species does not accept our God as their salvation, they follow other religions that distort the truth; or worse, they follow simply the religion of the individual." Bowman spoke that last part with a noticeable contempt and shook his head. "I've seen it all in my climb up the political ladder," he said, a note of disgust in his voice. "The backstabbing, the self-service, the true underlying greed of humanity bubbling just below the surface of your actions on a daily basis." He stopped directly in front of me and leaned in closely. "Do you know what I represent, boy?" he asked.

I leaned back a little in my chair, trying to keep as much distance from Bowman's face as possible. "They called you Conquest, but from what I recall," I said carefully, "the first Horseman represented pestilence."

Bowman looked visibly offended. "Sir, you insult me," he said curtly, straightening to his full height. "A cultural misunderstanding put forward by a novelist in the early twentieth century." He looked wistfully into the middle distance, as if remembering fond memories. "Conquest is a key obsession of humanity; money, fame, power, your entire culture is modelled around the conquest of these things. The religion of the individual is all about conquest, and that will be their downfall." He levelled his gaze back on me. "I offer you something else," he said.

I smirked a little. "To jump teams, I presume?" I observed.

"To accept redemption, my boy," Bowman said earnestly, leaning closer to my face. His eyes were gleaming with that same fanaticism I had seen on the podium earlier that evening. "A place in the new order." He grinned widely. "Soon I will usurp the President of this country," he said. "It will look like an attack from a foreign power, and I will use that to my advantage in pursuing my goals." He studied my expression carefully. "You have talents that are rarely found in the angelic hierarchy nowadays," he remarked. "You would be a valuable asset to us; you would finally make something out of your life."

I stiffened in the chair. "I have made something out of my life," I replied curtly.

Bowman smiled. "Really?" He asked. Suddenly the room around us began to fade and change, the darkness becoming brighter and twisting into new shapes and sounds. "You've been persecuted throughout your entire life, Sam," Bowman said, turning to look at the scene unfolding around us. "And not just your own life, but many others."

The scene around us swirled and fixed itself in place. I squinted around and caught my breath as I recognised the village square we were in, the wooden podium just in front of us and the man struggling against the ropes that bound him to the stake. The magistrate was just finishing reading the charges before the flames were lit. I closed my eyes, not wanting to see this again. "Stop it," I said.

Bowman smiled. "Uncomfortable to watch, isn't it? A man put to death for being different." I felt the world around us begin to shift again and I reopened my eyes. We were on a beach and I knew what was going to happen. I saw a man in the distance, coming closer, running as fast as he possibly could. His eyes were wide with panic and fear and I could hear his lungs heaving from even this distance. Behind him, horse-backed riders were charging in for the kill. I tried to close my eyes again, but something stopped me this time. Instead, I stared down at the man's terrified face as he tripped by the water's edge and sprawled defencelessly against his attackers. His lined, work-hardened Native American features were both foreign and yet awfully familiar. His eyes, the curl of his lips...

They were mine.

"What is this?" I demanded, staring wide-eyed at Bowman. "What are these dreams?"

Bowman smiled. "Memories, son," he said softly. "Memories of previous lives from your ancestral chain. You see, the angelic blood in you remembers. It's like a collective memory that stores up everything since your ancestor first betrayed his oath to the throne." Bowman looked over at the Native American, watching the downed man raising his hands in futile gesture against the cavalrymen sweeping in to kill him. "They've been resurfacing since you had close contact with the forces of Heaven again," he remarked. "And as you've seen, this world has treated you and your ancestors with nothing but fear and misunderstanding throughout the existence of your bloodline." Bowman turned to me again. "Right down to your current life," he said. "How long has it been since your wife left you?"

"Shut up," I said quietly, turning my head away.

Bowman shook his head sympathetically. "The fear, the misunderstanding and confusion that your abilities has caused you throughout your life," he said. "The bullying when you were young, the desperate attempts to keep your flashes of the future to yourself..."

"I said shut up!" I barked out at him, glaring with renewed hatred at my captor. My heart was pounding in my chest and I worked hard against the ropes that held me to the chair, but to no avail. "You don't know anything about my life!" I spat at him.

"Oh, but I do," Bowman said, his eyes gleaming. He leaned in closer to me. "I can see it all on the surface of your mind; I don't even need to push further." He crouched down next to my chair and whispered into my ear. "I can show you an alternative life, my boy," he breathed. "I can give you the respect and the privilege you deserve."

The scene around us began to fade, the Native American and his attackers dissolving. The beach around us shifted, transforming into rolling green pastures that spread out in all directions. We were now standing at the top of a hill, looking down across the beautiful greenery. I realised after a moment that this was the Garden of Eden again, very much as I had seen it when Norman and I had spoken the previous day. This time however, I could see further than before.

The rolling fields below us gradually began to transform into the urban sprawl of the Chicago downtown that I recognised, as if the fields of the garden had sprung up in the middle of the city and had pushed everything else to one side in order to fit. A brilliant light shone down from above, cleansing and purifying in its clarity, blinding me to the point that I had to shield my eyes. I heard a thousand voices singing in perfect harmony and saw a chorus of angels floating above the city, their halos of energy glowing an ethereal blue as they intoned their holy melodies. I saw massive statues rising up from the city, dwarfing even the largest skyscrapers; Adonis-like figures with immense wingspans reaching out in heroic poses towards unseen events and opportunities.

And right in the middle of them all, I saw one of myself.

Enormous to the point of breath-taking, cast in a bleach white marble that shone in the purifying sunlight from above as if it was the source of all power in the universe. I looked down and saw thousands upon thousands of worshippers at the foot of my statue, their voices intoning praise and fealty in perfect unison, whilst the choir of angels over their heads continued their beautiful song as if nothing else mattered in the world. It was breathtaking, and I had to remind myself to inhale. I sat there, not even bothering to fight against my restraints anymore, utterly dumbfounded by the majesty and joy of what I saw.

"You see what I can give you?" Bowman whispered, his voice like slow honey in my mind. "You see what difference you can make if you join our side? This is a war for the human soul, my son; this is war you want to be on the right side of. Help us get to the rebels and I will give you everything you have ever wanted."

I could not speak, my eyes transfixed on the immense scene before me. No more pain, no more fear of what people would think of me. The very thought of such a life was like utter bliss to my senses. No longer would I have to hide my abilities from people. I would be respected; loved and worshipped, in fact. No more being used as a thankless pawn by Alleam and his cronies to carry out the jobs they could not do. No more running. No more hiding.

Then, from nowhere, I felt an invisible hand touch my shoulder. "Remember what he can twist you to be," Norman's voice echoed in my brain. "What they all can twist you to be."

I blinked, the sudden memory cutting through the weariness and awe like a knife through butter. I shook my head a little, trying to formulate my thoughts. "Where is Miriam?" I asked.

Bowman, who had been staring down at the scene of things to come, looked around at me suddenly and blinked a couple of times. "What?" he asked.

"Where is Miriam?" I asked again. "You questioned her, and then what did you do with her?"

Bowman studied me for a long moment. "She was a traitor," he replied, his voice suddenly cold. "She betrayed her vows to God. There is no room for traitors and heathens in the Kingdom of Heaven." Bowman looked back out across the landscape, watching the angels dance above our heads. "She has gone to her punishment," he finished.

My heart went cold. I looked back out across the city before us, the chorus of the angels ringing in my ears, the murmurs of worshippers at the feet of enormous statues a constant background hum. "Slavery," I said quietly.

Bowman snapped his head around towards me. "What did you say?" he demanded.

"All I'm seeing is slavery," I said, turning to look Bowman in the eye. "Slavery, and a total, uncompromising denial of any other viewpoint than your own." My voice rose as I spoke, and I found myself becoming angry. I strained against the ropes that held me. "The worst kind of religious totalitarianism, dressed up as an eternal truth with no other way of life to be tolerated." I shook my head violently, my eyes boring into Bowman's own. "I won't be a part of it," I said. "I won't help consign billions to death for living their lives to the best of their abilities when their only crime is not believing in your boss!"

Bowman stared at me silently for a long moment. "What you're seeing is the future, son," he said softly. "What you're seeing is a portent of things to come. I'm offering you the chance to be on the right side of history; I would suggest you consider my offer very carefully."

I stared back at Bowman and smiled coldly. "I'm already

on the right side of history," I said. "No deal."

Bowman clucked his tongue, a look of disappointment on his face. "Very well," he said, turning away from me and walking a few steps. The scene in front of us faded away to leave the darkness of the warehouse once again. "I tried to help you, son," he said with a low voice. "I tried to show you the error of your ways." Bowman turned back to me, that fanatic gleam again in his eyes. "But your heretical beliefs will be punished, as will those of your compatriots." He reached out both hands towards me. I struggled in the chair, trying to push myself away to no avail. Bowman grinned unpleasantly at me. "I will have the information I need, Sam," he said. "And you will go to your judgement as a result."

"No!" I cried out, but there was nothing I could do. Bowman wrapped both hands around the sides of my head. A sharp, piercing pain shot through my scalp, an electric sensation that bored like a drill into my brain. I screamed, bucking against the ropes that held me, my feet kicking out uselessly.

But there was no escape.

I felt Bowman draw the information out of me as everything went white.

And then I died.

Chapter 16

I woke up.

I was in a room, desolate and bare. Metal walls betrayed flecks of paint from days of better ownership. A strip light flickered above my head, casting shadows into the corners of the room. I was sitting on a chair, an uncomfortable folding metal thing that creaked and threatened to collapse as I shifted my weight. A metal table stood in front of me, its surface bare apart from a chess set. Another chair faced me on the opposite side of the table. I was alone.

I looked around and realised with a sudden flash of panic that there was no door. Metal walls faced me on each side, oppressive and solid and offering no salvation. I stood shakily and walked around the table, studying each wall to see if there was some kind of hidden entrance. There was nothing I could see. I sat back down at the table again and put my head in my hands, desperately trying to lower my sense of panic and think logically.

The last thing I remembered was the searing pain in my head from Bowman's psychic assault. I shuddered at the memory; at least the pain had gone away. Wherever I was, I seemed to be away from the angels. That was a blessing at least; I just needed to find my way out. I wondered where Miriam was and how she was doing.

"She needs help," a smooth voice echoed from nowhere.

I jumped, looking around me frantically. "Who are you?" I demanded.

"I'm sorry, where are my manners," the voice replied again. I looked back to the table and jumped again; there was now a man sitting in the other chair, facing me. He was wearing a black shirt and tie, with a pair of dark grey suit trousers. His hair was short and business-like, his face angular and pale. His eyes were a dark, glowing red. When he spoke, it was with an upper-class English accent. "I'm terribly sorry," he said, smiling broadly. He had far too many teeth. "I sometimes forget that humans like to have a connection between what they see and what they hear." He cocked his head and smirked a little in amusement at his own comments. "Which is remarkably funny," he observed, "Given that most of humanity worship deities that they have never actually seen or heard in person."

I stared at the man, my muscles tensed against any kind of threat. "Who the hell are you?" I said again, my voice rising in pitch.

The man smiled again, as if I had said something funny. "Rather accurately put, my dear chap," he said with an amused tone. "In Hell, I am known as a Prince." He inclined his head politely. "Here on Earth, I am the President of the Los Hijos de la Parias. You may call me Beelzebub."

My heart leapt into my throat and I swallowed. Beelzebub watched me like a hawk watches its next meal and I suddenly felt the urge to move very slowly. "What do you want with me?" I asked, my tone softer than before.

Beelzebub smiled. "You're dead, Sam," he said, his voice as casual as if he was pointing out a stain on my shirt. "To put it bluntly, your soul was on its way to Hell and I intercepted it. We need to talk." Beelzebub's eyes glittered. "I need your help, Sam."

I had no idea what to say to that, so I stayed quiet. Beelzebub indicated the chess board in front of us, the pieces neatly lined up to begin a game. "Please," he said. "You move first."

I looked down at the board. I was indeed faced with the white pieces on my side of the board. I reached out, noticing that my hand was visibly trembling. I picked up a pawn from the centre of my army and, slowly, moved it forward two spaces. "How can I possibly help you?" I asked, watching him warily.

Beelzebub made a thoughtful noise, looking down at his own pieces. "We have a mutual interest, Sam," he said, reaching out one hand slowly towards his own pieces. "The end of the world and the beginning of the Apocalypse. Basically, we don't want to see this happen." He picked up one of his knights and lifted it up and across the front rank of his army to a position ahead of his pawns. "Your move," he said, leaning back in his chair.

I looked down at my pieces, contemplating my next move. My mind was racing; if Beelzebub needed my help with something, there was a chance that I could get out of here intact. I picked up one of my own knights and moved it in a similar fashion to Beelzebub. "For someone who doesn't want the world to end," I observed. "You're very much going along with it."

Beelzebub's eyes flashed briefly and I instantly regretted what I had said, wondering if I had pushed things too far. But then he merely inclined his head in acknowledgement. "I can see how it might look as such from an outsider's perspective," he conceded. "But there are larger forces at work here." He reached out and moved another piece. "We're bound by promises made long before you were born to co-operate with Heaven's wishes to initiate the Apocalypse."

I frowned. "I'm not getting that," I said, reaching out to move another pawn. "Aren't you guys supposed to be mortal enemies, fighting for the souls of humanity?"

Beelzebub nodded. "We are, but things are more complicated than that," he said, matching my move by taking one of my pieces. I flinched a little in expectation of some kind of punishment, but nothing happened. Beelzebub took the fallen piece and placed it neatly along one end of his side of the table. "When Lucifer staged his revolution," Beelzebub explained, looking up at me. "He was defeated. Instead of himself and his allies being wiped from existence, God put them to work as his prison guards." He nodded at the board. "Your move, dear boy."

I looked down at the board and moved another piece. "Prison guards?" I asked. "I'm not following you."

Beelzebub smiled. "Who do you think created Hell?" he asked, reaching towards one of his own pieces. "God, of course; he created everything, after all." He took another of my pieces. "Before Hell, unbelievers simply vanished into non-existence. After Lucifer's rebellion, God had another idea; create a place of eternal damnation for those who work against His will, and have those who fell from grace as both inmates and guards. "He smiled. "God allows Lucifer's forces to walk upon Earth, to corrupt the people He created in order to test their loyalties. Those that fail are cast down to Hell."

I stared at Beelzebub, the game forgotten. "That's horrendous," I said.

Beelzebub shrugged. "It keeps us in a job," he replied casually. "But we've obviously been doing our job too well, because Heaven has invoked the Treaty of Revelation."

"I've heard of that," I said, looking back down at the board. Beelzebub's pieces were working their way up the middle of the board and my own pieces were in danger of being split into two. I retreated the Knight I had moved earlier for safety's sake. "So far as I understand it," I continued, "Revelation is actually some kind of agreed blueprint for the end of the world."

Beelzebub nodded. "That's correct," he said, an approving smile on his face. "We have to go through the initial stages of the Apocalypse without interfering; this includes the work of the Four Horsemen." He reached out and moved his Queen into play. "However, once Heaven unleashes its punishments across the Earth and rescue the forty-four thousand truly faithful, we have the chance to meet Heaven in battle."

I frowned. "If I recall correctly, Hell is defeated in that battle," I observed.

Beelzebub waved a hand dismissively. "Religious propaganda put out by the early church leaders," he said. "The final battle is undecided; if the forces of Hell win, we take custody of the Earth and all of those who remain after the forty-four thousand are taken to Heaven." Beelzebub nodded to the board, reminding me that it was my move.

I moved a piece, but I was not really paying attention. My mind was spinning. "But you have to wait until this final battle to do anything," I said, running the chronology of what he was saying through my head.

Beelzebub nodded. "Exactly," he said. "Until then, we are relegated to observation." He reached out and took another one of my pieces. My side of the board was starting to look noticeably sparse. "The treaty allows us to have a delegation on Earth to monitor the movements of Heaven and to make sure they're sticking to their side of the bargain," he continued. "However, we're restricted in numbers to be equal to the Heavenly delegation until the final battle. We're also forbidden from any overt actions against Heaven until then."

I looked up at him and raised an eyebrow. "Your agents have tried to kill me," I observed. "You've engaged in a massive digging operation to uncover a supernatural super-weapon and you've interrupted the passage of my soul after I was apparently killed by a Horseman of the Apocalypse." I leaned back in my chair. "You're not exactly sticking to the letter of the law, are you?"

Beelzebub smiled and shrugged slightly. "We behave much as your terrestrial governments do," he said dismissively. "Sometimes we have to go against the letter of the law to protect our own interests." He leaned forward, locking his eyes on mine with an intensity that made me very uncomfortable. "We have no desire to see the end of the world," he said earnestly. "And we have no problem being…flexible with our agreements with Heaven." He tilted his head a little in a gesture of acknowledgement to some self-evident truth. "However, we cannot be seen to overtly work against Heaven," he said. "Our forces are not powerful enough yet to initiate the final battle we yearn for." A wave of irritation flickered across his face. "Unfortunately," he added, "I am having an issue selling that idea to some of my underlings."

I quirked a smile. "Trouble in paradise?" I asked.

Beelzebub smiled broadly at me and the sight of so many teeth wiped my own smile away. "We're having a slight problem with discipline," he said. "My second-in-command, Astartoth; I believe you have met?"

I grunted, remembering the events at the quarry. "We've run into each other before, yes," I replied with a mock casualness.

Beelzebub nodded. "It was forces loyal to Astartoth that tried to capture you, Sam; not kill," he said. "It was an unauthorised move, for which I apologise." I blinked in surprise at that and he smiled. "I can be magnanimous when I am wrong," he said. "I have dissension in my ranks; the small group of forces around Astartoth want to start the final battle with Heaven now; none of this waiting for the Apocalypse to unfold, they want me to strike with the element of surprise."

"And you think it's a bad idea," I observed.

Beelzebub grimaced. "They are fools," he said. "We are not ready. Astartoth disagreed with me and went off behind my back trying to capture you and dig up the Ophanim to use against me." He shook his head wistfully. "He has too much support for me to just get rid of him, and he has the ear of Lucifer himself. I have to work behind the scenes to discredit him." Beelzebub smiled. "Thank-you for taking care of that Ophanim issue for me," he said.

I frowned. "What did that have to do with you?" I asked.

Beelzebub looked at me for a long moment. My mind whirred for a few moments and then stopped when I hit the answer. My mouth dropped open. "We got the information on the dig from Furcas," I said.

Beelzebub nodded. "Furcas was working with Astartoth," he acknowledged. "He organised the security for the dig site."

I looked at the fallen angel for a long moment, not quite believing what I was thinking. "You told Alleam where to find Furcas," I said slowly. "You hung him out to dry so that we would get the information, stop Astartoth getting the Ophanim and solve your problem for you."

Beelzebub merely smiled. "Your move," he said, nodding to the board.

I looked down. He had my forces boxed in from various angles and was poised to take my King. I moved a piece to block the obvious path he had set up, trying to buy time in more ways than one. "So what do you want from me now?" I asked.

Beelzebub's eyes glinted. "I'm going to set you free, Sam," he said. "I'm also going to offer you the assistance of the forces at my disposal in stopping the Horseman of Conquest; covertly, of course." He leaned forward again. "In return for which," he said, his voice low and filled with soft menace. "You're going to owe me a favour."

I pursed my lips. "You think I'm a complete idiot?" I said, folding my arms. "Get into bed with the Lord of the Flies?" I shook my head. "No deal."

Beelzebub's smile faltered. "Consider the facts, Sam," he said. "You're dead and so is your compatriot, the nun." He smiled at my expression of alarm. "Yes," he said. "She passed through before you and is currently a guest of my colleagues in the city of Dis." He opened both hands to me, palms out in an expressive gesture. "I can help you get her back, Sam," he said. "And then I can send you back to your own world to save your species from oblivion. Alternatively, you can burn in the fires of Hell with some of the worst members of society that have ever existed, whilst everything you know and love above your head burns in the upcoming war." With a flourish, he reached out to a piece on the chess board, moved it and then looked back up at me. "Check mate," he said.

I sat for a long moment, staring at the board. He was right; I had to either agree to help him or spend the rest of eternity in torment. To say the choice was one-sided was putting it lightly. I sighed, my shoulders slumping in a gesture of defeat, and nodded slowly. "Deal," I said quietly. Then I looked up. "So how do I get Miriam?" I asked.

Beelzebub smiled again, pushing his chair back from the table. "I will send you there personally," he said. "I'll give you the chance of a return ticket; not something that many people who enter our realm get." He tilted his head. "You might even come out of this alive." His eyes narrowed. "Do not disappoint me, Sam," he said quietly.

I went to reply but could think of nothing to say. Beelzebub flicked his hand in a gesture and the room began to fade around me. I felt myself sinking into darkness and braced myself for what was to come.

I have been told many times in my life to go to Hell. I never thought I would be making a flying visit.

Chapter 17

After what seemed like an eternity in the strange, weightless place of nothingness I drifted through, the darkness around me began to brighten. I squinted, discerning shapes in the distance as the world around me reformed. The light was different; instead of the cleansing brightness of sunlight, hues of fiery red and glowing orange lit up my surroundings. I suddenly felt solid ground beneath my feet and blinked a few times as the world came into focus.

I was at the edge of a river, the dark waters lapping at my feet just to my left. The river stretched on as far as I could see, arcing gently to the right until it disappeared from view behind an immense stone wall. The wall was hundreds of feet high, towering over me like a slumbering monster, its decaying façade pockmarked with battlements and guard towers that gazed upon me accusingly. Fires flared from countless lamps on the lower edges of the walls, casting an eerie glow onto the ground on which I stood. I could see a massive, fortified gate not far from where I stood, its iron bars foreboding. A huge, stone plaque dominated the space above the gate, the name of the city chipped into it in crooked indents.

The City of Dis.

I heard a cry of alarm from the battlements and looked up. I had been spotted. A bright light leapt from the wall and arced down towards me at high speed. It slammed into me before I could react, sending me flying sideways. I rolled several times, managing to stop myself just before rolling into the dark waters of the river. Scrabbling to my feet, my hands slipping on the stony ground, I turned to face whatever had hit me.

The fallen angel stood in front of me, her outline illuminated with the blood red aura that I was getting so used to seeing around the servants of Hell. She stared at me coldly from behind red eyes, her shock of black hair at odds with the gleaming silver of her armour. She gripped a long, sharp sword in one hand and she tensed as I turned to face her. "I am Tisiphone," she said grandly. "One of the furies; those that guard the gates of Dis." She cocked her head at me, scrutinising me with a dark expression. "And you," she sneered. "Are a spy from Heaven."

I held up both hands in supplication. "Wrong idea," I said carefully, my eyes searching to see if she was about to make a move. "I'm just here to get somebody back that doesn't belong here, that's all."

Tisiphone spat. Her spittle hit the ground and sizzled. "Liar," she snarled at me, bringing the sword up in her grasp. "Nobody gets to the city walls without crossing the Styx first, and we would have been aware of that. You must have been sent here by Heavenly means."

I shook my head. "I'm here thanks to your boss, Beelzebub," I said. "He sent me down here, nobody else."

Tisiphone laughed; it was a soul-chilling cackle that bounced off the walls of the city and filled the air from all directions. "A ridiculous story," she said. "We have been told nothing." Her eyes narrowed and I saw her legs tense up. "Now die, traitorous spy!" she snarled.

"Wait!" I shouted, but it was too late. Tisiphone leapt at me and I threw myself to one side. She blew past me like a missile, charging out over the waters of the Styx before arcing back around in my direction. I heard another cry and spun around. From the walls of Dis, another two red lights were charging down towards me; more of Tisiphone's fellow furies, I presumed. I was being honed in on from three different directions. There was no way I could defend myself from all three.

I was suddenly blinded by a flash of brilliant, white

light. It appeared out of nowhere in front of me, hanging in the air before launching itself away at blistering speed. It slammed into the furies' own red aura and sent it flying away in a drunken fashion. I heard the painful screech of Tisiphone. I watched as the white light turned and launched itself towards the second fury. It slammed into them with much the same effect, sending the guardian of Dis careening into the waters of the Styx and out of sight under its murky, black surface.

The third fury almost stopped in mid-air, hesitating after seeing what happened to the other two. As the white light turned in their direction, this fury obviously thought better of the attack and retreated, arcing over and back towards the walls of Dis like a wounded bird heading for a nest. The light turned back towards me and slowly came to a halt in front of me. I smiled, stepping forward. "Thanks, Anahita," I said, genuine relief in my voice.

The white light dimmed, turning gradually red. Eventually it dissipated entirely and my smile fell away. The angel was a man, dressed in full battle armour and clutching a broadsword in his gauntlet-covered hands. His hair was long and black, trailing down almost to his waist and flowing in an unfelt breeze. His red eyes were hard and his mouth was set in a grim line within a large, black beard. He surveyed me for a few moments without saying a word, and for a moment I thought he was going to strike. Then he bowed his head ceremoniously to me and said, "My greetings to you, my Lord."

I blinked, unsure of how to handle this. "Who are you?" I said.

The angel's eyes flicked up to mine; he was judging my every word, I realised. "I am Asmodeus," he said, lifting his chin proudly. "Lord of Hell, Demon of Lust, Commander of the 72 Legions." He pursed his lips. "And your guardian, as stipulated by my Lord Beelzebub," he said, a hint of irritation in his voice.

I raised my brow. "My guardian?" I asked incredulously. "Beelzebub never said anything about a babysitter."

Asmodeus' eyes narrowed. "Nonetheless, it is so," he replied, staring me directly in the eyes. "I have been tasked to protect you through the city of Dis and after your return to the surface. You have no choice in the matter."

I opened my mouth to argue, but considered my position; I was standing alone at the edge of a demon-infested city in the middle of literal Hell. My shoulders sagged in defeat. "Alright," I said quietly. "How do we get inside?"

Asmodeus merely smiled. "Like this," he said, and he turned towards the gate. He threw both hands forward and, with much obvious effort, swept them both aside as if parting the fabric of the world. I saw the gates shudder, several large stones and debris crashing down from the battlements. A piercing squeal of metal gears made me cover my ears as I saw the huge gates begin to open. Beyond them, I saw nothing but fire. My heart leapt into my throat and I almost shuddered in fear, but I noticed Asmodeus watching me closely. These fallen angels seemed to respect strength above all else, so I forced myself to sound calm as I said, "Alright, let's get on with this." I strode toward the gates, ignoring the fear in my gut and the looming shadow of the fallen angel at my shoulder.

We walked through the gates of the City of Dis. My mouth dropped open and my mind started to scream, but I kept my face neutral and my eyes fixed straight ahead. We walked down the road, the ground lined with uneven and dirtied cobblestones that were dark with soot. To either side, tombs stretched on as far as the eye could see. Each one was in flames. Asmodeus walked beside me, his eyes roving the horizon for threats. There was nobody else on the street, but from each tomb I heard the horrific sound of agonised screaming. "What is the purpose of all of this?" I asked, a lump in my throat making it hard to talk.

Asmodeus answered without looking at me. "This is the Sixth Circle of Hell, my Lord," he answered. "This is where heretics are sentenced to burn for eternity in open tombs."

I had nothing to say in response to that, so we walked in silence and I desperately tried to keep the sound of screams out of my head. We continued for what seemed like an eternity, the tombs on either side never stopping, until we reached a point where the road ended abruptly. The ground dropped away without warning into a sheer cliff. I edged closer and looked over; below, I could see several concentric circles of land, each level a sheer drop from the one above and each one filled with horrors beyond imagination. The lowest level was barely visible, but appeared to be covered in ice. I could see something there, something huge. It growled and I felt the noise in my skull. I shuddered and stepped back from the edge quickly.

Asmodeus was studying the nearby tombs. "That one," he said, pointing at one large entrance. The doorway was filled with flames. Unusually, I could hear nothing from inside. Asmodeus turned to look at me. "Your friend is inside," he said. "We must recover her quickly before-"

He was interrupted by a blood-curdling roar from the direction of the city gates. This time, it was a scream of rage rather than anguish. We both looked around to see bright flashes of red heading in our direction. "Looks like the furies found their nerve," I remarked, looking over at Asmodeus.

The fallen angel stared at the oncoming threat and took a step forward. "They are not alone," he said, drawing his sword out in front of him. It hummed with an energy that made my spine prickle. "They have Innana with them."

My heart skipped a beat. "Great," I breathed.

Asmodeus looked over at me. "You have met?" he enquired.

I nodded. "We've bumped into each-other before," I said with forced nonchalance. "It looks like the furies are siding with Astartoth in this little Civil War you've got brewing."

Asmodeus nodded. "So it would seem," he agreed, adjusting to a fighting stance. "Get your friend and get ready to leave," he said, his eyes never leaving the incoming attackers.

I gestured emphatically at the tomb. "How am I supposed to get through that?" I asked.

Asmodeus glanced at me. "If you're as worthy as my Lord Beelzebub seems to think," he replied, "then you will find a way." And with that, he launched himself into the air at breakneck speed, leaving a trail of red energy behind him.

I watched him arcing up towards Innana and the furies, wondering if he was powerful enough to do the job. Then I turned away and ran towards the tomb, my mind racing. I stopped just short of the flames, straining to see past their burning tips into the darkness beyond. I could see a stone table upon which a body lay. The entire inside of the tomb was in flames as well. I had no idea where Miriam was or if she was even still alive, but I had to find a way. I pushed forward, hoping that I could somehow squeeze around the fire, but it seemed to rise towards me with every movement I made as if aware of my trying to pass. I stepped back, thinking hard. I looked back over my shoulder towards the city gates, towards the waters beyond.

In my mind's eye, I heard Gemma's voice from the diner. "You just sort of – it's hard to describe- you just sort of focus on what you want to happen in your mind's eye and let it happen."

Flashes of light above my head made me look up; the streaks of red light that denoted the fallen angels were slamming into each other, flashing and crackling with an intensity of energy that made me blink away after-images from my eyes. I saw one streak nimbly, darting between the others; Asmodeus, I presumed. He seemed to be holding his own, but I had no idea for how long that would last. I took a deep breath. This was my only shot; I had to try it. I closed my eyes, stretching my hands out towards the gates of the city and imagining myself reaching for the waters beyond. In my mind's eye, I felt the water, cold and slimy, against the palms of my hands. Then I lifted my arms and brought them towards me with a violent gesture.

There was an enormous rumble, and I felt the ground shudder beneath my feet. Through the open gates in the distance, I saw the waters of the Styx rise in a whirling funnel, arcing up and towards me like a giant, shifting snake. The waters flew towards me, and at the gesture of my hands I redirected the funnel at the front of Miriam's tomb. The water crashed into the flames with a hiss like a thousand serpents. A huge cloud of steam rose and rolled away from the tomb, temporarily blinding me. I groped my way forward through the mist, tripping over the uneven stones beneath my feet. I found the entrance to the tomb and stumbled in, the massive stench of rot and decay making me gag. I covered my mouth with one hand and tried to keep my breathing as shallow as my pounding heart allowed. Through the gloom of the tomb's interior, I ran across to the slab upon which the body lay. It was Miriam. She was seemingly unconscious, her chest rising and falling slowly. She appeared physically unscathed from the flames, although the tortured look on her face suggested immense pain. I scooped her up carefully in my arms and lifted her off the slab, walking as fast I could out of the tomb without dropping her.

Asmodeus was still high above us, his fiery red outline streaking across the sky with a grace and poise that I could barely follow. He twisted and turned skilfully around the other glowing entities that made up Innana and the furies, all of whom were darting and angling around each other in his wake with a frantic and jerking attitude to their movements. They were clearly frustrated at not being able to take him down. I saw powerful balls of energy blast forward from the outlines of Asmodeus' pursuers, which he skilfully avoided with a twist in direction and a sudden dive down towards the city. He adjusted his trajectory and I realised that he was heading right towards us. I flinched instinctively at the oncoming threat, Miriam still unconscious in my hands. Asmodeus suddenly braked in his descent and landed in a crouch on the ground in front of me, the red aura around his body coalescing momentarily into the outlines of massive wings behind his back. He stood and braced his sword in one hand, turning away from us to look at the sky. The furies and Innana were speeding in earnest towards our location. More balls of energy shot forward. Asmodeus swung his sword across his body and intercepted one of them, sending it careening away across the city's horizon. He hit another energy ball and it crashed into a nearby tomb with a roaring explosion that sent decayed marble and stone flying like shrapnel.

"Any time you'd like to leave, I'm good with it," I panted, the unconscious Miriam heavy in my arms. My heart was pounding as I watched the incoming furies nervously.

Asmodeus turned to look at me and quirked a smile. "What's the matter, my Lord?" he said with mock courtesy. "Not feeling like a little exercise in hand-to-hand combat?"

I glared at him. "This may sound surprising, but I'd rather keep my mortality intact than stay down here with your friends for the rest of eternity," I said sarcastically.

Asmodeus shrugged, looking back around at the furies. "As you wish, my Lord," he said with a tone of amusement. He reached out a hand to me without looking back. "Hold on tight," he said, narrowing his eyes.

I shifted Miriam into a Fireman's hold over one shoulder and took Asmodeus' hand in my own. His skin was ice cold, and I felt a constant electric-like current that made my arm erupt in goose bumps. I saw him glance back at me, bend his legs in a slight crouch…

…and we were airborne.

I hung on for dear life as we rocketed upwards, the red glow of energy surrounding us and clouding my vision so that I could barely see. The wind whipped past us at increasing speed as I held as tightly onto Miriam as I could. The scenery around us became a blur as we sped faster upwards, concentric rings of land shooting past us. The sky above us grew lighter and I heard Innana scream in frustration from below, her high pitched anger echoing like a wild beast denied its prey. I looked down and saw her and the furies being left further and further behind, until their glowing red forms were merely pinpricks in my vision. I grinned ferociously, looking back up at the sky as the brightness grew with every second until everything became white.

☦

I gasped for air and opened my eyes, blinking furiously. I was in total darkness and the air was stale, but every breath felt like sweet honey in my mouth. I groped out blindly, finding my hands stopping a foot away from my face against something hard. It felt like wood; I braced my hands and feet against it and pushed with all my might. The air was getting warm and I found my breathing getting heavier; I realised with a panic that there was very little oxygen in this enclosed space. I grunted with exertion and felt the wood begin to give, cracking and splintering as it did. A thin ray of gloomy light shone in through one of the cracks and I hammered my hands against it, forcing a larger hole. With a resounding crack, the wood gave way in the centre and I sat up with a huge gasp of air. I was in a large, plain wooden coffin, half buried in the side of a massive industrial landfill. All I could see on all sides were mountains of rusting vehicles, machines and white goods, their metallic surfaces gleaming in the moonlight above me. I pulled myself out of the coffin and onto the side of the mountain, struggling to keep my balance over twisted fenders and discarded sheet metal. I saw another coffin only a few feet away and stumbled across, still trying to get my breath. I leaned against it and could hear a scratching noise from within. With a grunt, I gripped the corners of the lid and heaved with all my strength. After a moment, the wood broke and the lid swung up and over with a violent noise. Miriam sat up within, heaving for breath and looking around in confusion. "What...?" she mumbled, obviously disoriented.

I took her gently by both shoulders and helped her out. "Are you okay?" I asked, looking her in the eyes.

"I...don't know," she muttered, wrapping her arms around her torso. Then she shivered. "The fire," she murmured, looking away into the middle distance.

I shook her gently. "Stay with me," I said gently. "We'll get you to safety." I looked around and took a deep breath. "Anahita!" I shouted.

There was a sudden flash of blue light, and my guardian angel was standing in front of me. She looked worried and she reached out for my arm with genuine concern. "Thank God," she said to herself. "I've been searching for you everywhere. Are you two okay?"

"We took a detour," I replied, rubbing my head absently. I ached all over and the after-images of Dis swam just behind my eyes. I suddenly wondered what had happened to Asmodeus and I looked around. I could not see him anywhere, but I felt something present nearby. I shook my head to clear it and looked over at Miriam. "We need to get her to safety," I said in a low voice to Anahita. "And I need to see Alleam."

Anahita nodded, her eyes full of worry. "What are we going to do?" she whispered.

I stood up, my muscles screaming from the exertion, but I ignored the pain. I looked out across the mounds of garbage, towards the lights of Chicago in the distance. "I know who the Horseman is," I said grimly, my eyes locked on the city. "And I'm going to stop him."

Chapter 18

Anahita transported Miriam and me away from the landfill site shortly afterwards. We dropped Miriam off at Norman's commune; the Warden – the same long-haired man who had met us before – took her into their care and promised that they would look after her wounds. I could not see anything physically wrong with her, but from the way she stumbled as she walked into the building and the constantly dazed look on her face I feared that Miriam was hurting dramatically on the inside. She had been through an experience that very few people had ever survived in folklore; I was sure that she was not okay.

Anahita then took me straight to Alleam. We met him at a gas station on the outskirts of Chicago, the night above us now in full command of the sky. Alleam was standing in the half-illumination of a red neon sign that proclaimed prices to passing motorists. As we re-materialised, he walked towards us with a grim look on his face. I leaned on Anahita, my muscles aching as if I had run a marathon. It seemed that my soul's visit to Hell had an adverse effect on my body as well; something I found rather disconcerting. Alleam looked at me for a long moment before speaking. "Well?" he said, his voice full of tension.

I blinked. "Well?" I parroted. "That's all you've got to say?" I let go of Anahita and forced myself to stand upright on my own. "I've just been through Hell for you; the actual Hell!" I snapped, jabbing my finger at Alleam accusingly. "No words of concern for my wellbeing, or questions about Miriam's health?" I shook my head in disgust. "How do you even get people to work with you?" I asked.

Alleam glared at me and I saw his eyes turning brighter. "We have far more important things to worry about than your own skin," he retorted, clenching his fists with anger. "Who is the Horseman?"

So I told him; how the Horseman was the Vice President of the United States, how he had managed to get the identities of Alleam and Anahita from my mind by force, and how Miriam and I had been sent to Hell. I left out Asmodeus as I did not know what reaction Alleam may have, simply telling him that we blacked out after I rescued Miriam and woke up on the landfill. I did have to tell him about Beelzebub and how I now owed him for his assistance in rescuing Miriam. The stunned silence resonated around the empty gas station for several minutes before anyone said anything. "Very well," Alleam said, nodding slightly. "Then we take out the Vice President."

I looked at him incredulously. "This isn't some biker-faking angel that can't really get their hands dirty in the real world for fear of exposure," I retorted, spreading my arms wide in exasperation. "We're talking about the Vice-President of the most powerful country on the planet, surrounded by Secret Service personnel – some of whom are in on the plot – and a massive number of regular police officers." I glanced between both of them. "All of whom will be armed, and all of whom have the full permission of the authorities to open fire on anything they deem a threat." I shook my head. "He's likely got angelic support as well; this seems like we're walking into a shooting range."

Alleam shook his head. "It is of no concern to us," he replied. "We are here to stop the Apocalypse; everything else is secondary."

I smirked. "The ends justify the means, do they?" I replied. "Which side are you on again?"

Alleam blinked at me. "What do you mean?"

I folded my arms. "You seem rather cavalier about throwing away the lives that you are here to protect," I replied. "Many of those people protecting the Vice President will be simply doing their jobs with no fathom of what is actually going on and you're more than happy to kill them in order to achieve your ends." I shook my head slowly. "That doesn't exactly sound very holy to me."

Alleam took a step closer to me. "Given that you are now in league with the arch-enemy of Mankind," he said in a quiet, dangerous voice, "I would counsel you against questioning my motives." He looked down his nose at me. "You're just another foolish, unrighteous specimen that is more than happy to consign yourself to owing favours to the Devil in order to get what you want." He snorted. "No wonder Heaven is calling down the Apocalypse," he said with a disgusted tone. "I sometimes think we might as well let them get on with it."

I laughed aloud, turning and walking away a few paces. "Oh no, you don't get to pull the pious angel routine now," I spat back, turning back to face him. "You turned your back on your own kind because you wanted to stop innocent people from dying, and that means that you yourself have got into bed with some horrible people too in order to make that happen."

Alleam lifted his chin in an aloof manner. "I have no idea what you're talking about," he said stiffly.

I sneered at him. "Beelzebub told me about your little deal regarding Furcas," I said. "He told you where to find him, in return for which you took care of his Ophanim problem for him."

Alleam stiffened. "We needed that Ophanim to take out the Horseman," he said calmly, although I sensed a little less righteousness in his voice this time.

I smiled. "Yeah, and Beelzebub is rather delighted to have it out of Astartoth's hands so he can keep his place at the top of the totem pole here on Earth," I observed. "And yet you were happy to help him with that little issue if it got you what you wanted." I folded my arms. "So tell me," I replied tersely. "How exactly are you any better than me?"

The silence lengthened into the night, the distant noises of Chicago the only sounds. Alleam and I glared at each other, neither one speaking. Eventually, Alleam turned away, staring into the darkness. Anahita stepped forward, looking between the two of us carefully. "So what do we do?" she asked. "We still have a Horseman to stop."

I replied to Anahita without taking my eyes of Alleam's back. "We take Beelzebub's offer of help," I said.

"No!" Alleam snapped, turning back to glare at me. "We do not involve him in this!"

"If you've got a better idea, I'd like to hear it!" I retorted.

Alleam did not have a response, merely pursing his lips. Eventually he sighed. "He has given you a way to contact him?" he said, an air of resigned disgust underlying his tone.

I nodded, thinking of Asmodeus. "Yes," I replied. "And we need to hurry." I looked between the two angels in front of me. "I've got a plan," I said.

Chapter 19

The Peninsula was a large, imposing structure in downtown Chicago, brightly-lit and ostentatious against the glowing skyline of the Chicago night. A five-star hotel, it played host to the wealthiest of visitors, but today it was even harder to get to than usual. The Peninsula was where both the President and Vice President of the United States would be staying during their visit to Chicago. The front of the hotel was ringed with police and barricades, preventing casual onlookers from getting too close to the front of the building. Only Bowman was currently in the hotel – the President was flying in later that day – but security was already incredibly tight in anticipation.

From where we stood further down the block from the Peninsula, hidden in the shadows that the night provided, it looked impregnable. That was good; it would hopefully make them even more surprised when we broke in.

I was standing at the corner of the street, watching the building quietly. "This is going to be one hell of a fireworks show," I remarked.

I could not see it happen, but I felt Asmodeus melt into being over my left shoulder. The Lord of Hell nodded, his eyes observing the front of the building critically. "Fortunately, we're good at making hell," he remarked. Then he glanced at me. "You did not tell Alleam or your guardian angel about me," he observed.

It was not a question, but I nodded anyway. "I didn't think it was a good idea to mention you after I only narrowly got a pass from asking Beelzebub to do us a favour here," I remarked.

Asmodeus nodded. "A wise idea," he said, and I could have sworn for a moment that I heard an air of satisfaction in his voice. "So what did you tell them about your side of this plan?"

"That I would be accompanied temporarily by a representative from Hell's forces," I replied. "Nothing more permanent than that." I glanced over at Asmodeus. "Are your forces in position?" I asked.

Asmodeus nodded. "Ready when you are, my Lord," he replied.

I nodded grimly. "Alright," I said, tensing up slightly in anticipation. "Let's get this over with."

Asmodeus nodded and closed his eyes, going completely still. I felt the hairs on the back of my neck prickle as if I was standing too close to an electrical current. After a moment he opened his eyes again and nodded. "It is done," he said.

I turned to watch. Within minutes, the roar of engines could be heard on the horizon. I saw the police and security agents outside the hotel stir into activity at the sudden noises, looking either way up the street with apprehension. The engines grew to a cacophony that seemed to drown out all other noise, and the convoy of bikers in un-patched jackets turned onto the closed street in front of the Peninsula. They mounted the pavements and blew through the barriers, screeching to a halt across the street from the hotel.

And then they opened up with literal Hellfire.

Beams of red light, searing my retinas with their luminosity, leaped the distance between the hands of the infernal bikers and the front of the hotel, striking at the façade, smashing windows and doors as they did. Blazes of twisting fire, swirling like vortexes, lit up the night sky as they seared the pavement in front of the hotel and sent panicked law enforcement and secret service agents diving for cover. Return fire began sporadically from the security forces that had recovered from the initial assault, but the bullets seemed to curve away and miss the bikers at every point. I watched with awestruck horror as the infernal bikers sat in a seemingly invulnerable bubble, unleashing horrendous energy against the front of the hotel.

This was what the end of the world would look like, I realised.

Asmodeus was already moving. "We need to go!" he shouted. We sprinted across the street and along the road, running parallel to the hotel. The majority of the security forces were scrambling towards the front of the hotel, and amidst the chaos we managed to reach the building. A side exit marked 'Loading Dock Office' was our way in and Asmodeus sent it flying off its hinges with a brief blast of energy. A couple of Secret Service agents spun around and took aim towards us. I was half-way through the doorway when I saw them and froze, but Asmodeus roughly pushed me to one side and took the brunt of the bullets from the agent's weapons. Whether they even hit him or not I could not tell, but a brief blast of energy lanced out from Asmodeus' hands and sent the two agents flying backwards across the room. They landed unconscious against the rear wall and Asmodeus advanced on them, his hands crackling with glowing red energy.

I grabbed him by the shoulder. "No!" I hissed. "We're not killing anyone we don't have to."

The Lord of Hell turned to me with a look bordering on puzzlement. "Very well," he said lowering his hands, the energy around them rescinding to a low-level glow. "Lead the way," he said, indicating the door at the far end of the building.

We stormed through the door and into the stairwell beyond. I initially went for the stairs, but Asmodeus stopped me and indicated to hold onto him. I wrapped one arm around his neck and we were lifting into the air at a rapid pace, the staircase climbing around us in a dizzying fashion. "The Horseman?" Asmodeus asked me as we rose, keeping his eye on the entrances to the stairwell as we flew past them.

I closed my eyes, letting my Second Sight take hold. I felt myself floating away from my already moving body in a gut churning moment of disorientation. I focused on Bowman, searching for him within the building. I found him within a few moments; he was being roused from bed by two desperate looking Secret

Service agents. They were bundling him out of the door into the corridor and into a service elevator, which started moving downwards. "He's on the move," I said from, my eyes clenched closed. "He's heading for the back entrance as anticipated."

Asmodeus nodded. "I hope your compatriot is in position," he shouted back to me.

Alleam was. I watched from my extra-bodily position as the elevator opened on the ground floor near the rear of the hotel's maintenance and laundry facilities. He let loose with a volley of blinding blue light at the carriage, scouring the rear wall of the elevator and forcing Bowman and his entourage to press themselves to the walls in order to avoid being incinerated. I saw one of the agents punch the button for the roof and I allowed myself a feeling of celebration. "They're heading for the helicopter pad," I shouted to Asmodeus, opening my eyes again.

Asmodeus grinned widely. "We'll get there first," he shouted, and I felt us increase speed. I could not help but grin as well; everything was going according to plan.

The blast of blue light that almost skewered me through the torso, however, was unexpected.

The angel was wearing the same suit and dark glasses as the Secret Service agents we had seen outside the building. Asmodeus had managed to arc us around the shot with a move so swift that it left my stomach in my feet. We landed unceremoniously on the staircase and hit the deck, the blue beams of light shooting over us and impacting the walls around the stairwell. I turned to look at Asmodeus. "We're going to get cooked if we stay here much longer!" I shouted.

Asmodeus nodded, glancing up the stairwell. "We are only a few floors from the roof," he replied, ducking his head to avoid another blast of energy. "I will hold this one back; you keep going."

"How the hell am I supposed to take on a Horseman of the Apocalypse on my own?" I shouted back.

"You just need to stall him!" snarled Asmodeus, rising to his feet in between the angel's shots and beginning to fire back. Blue and red energy lanced across the stairwell as each duellist ducked and weaved around each other's shots. "Go, quickly!" He shouted to me. Keeping my head low, I ran blindly up the staircase, trying to keep my profile as low as possible in case the angel decided to take a shot at me instead. Asmodeus seemed to be keeping him appropriately distracted however, and a few minutes later I burst through the door onto the rooftop of the Peninsula and looked around.

The roof of the hotel was normally decked out as an outside drinking and eating area, with chairs and tables set underneath elegant gazebos and surrounded by flowers and water features. I knew this because I had seen it previously in television adverts. Now however, the entire area had been cleared away and reinforced, with a helicopter parked neatly at one end of the roof. A couple of Secret Service agents were crouched nearby the helicopter with guns drawn, ready for any potential incursion by attackers on the Vice President's secondary escape route.

They opened fire as soon as I stumbled through the door and I only just managed to throw myself behind a low brick wall, the bullets zipping by my head as I dove. I hit the concrete with a grunt and rolled onto my back, trying to catch my breath. I knew without using my Second Sight that the agents would be moving up on my position to take care of the threat before the Vice President arrived, and I needed to do something fast.

There was a line of heavy, ceramic plant pots lining the top of the wall; I focused on them with my mind's eye and threw my hands outwards in a throwing gesture. The pots launched themselves from the wall in various directions; I heard several smashes and two pained grunts. I lifted my head tentatively and saw both agents lying on their backs on either side of the rooftop, obviously having tried to move around to flank me on both sides. That threat taken care of, all I had to do now was deal with

Bowman for a little while and keep him on the roof. I screwed my eyes closed and concentrated on my Second Sight, detaching my mind from my body and floating up above the wall to see beyond my protective barrier. It was strange, seeing my own body curled up on the floor, but I forced myself to ignore the dissonance and concentrate on the elevator doors, awaiting Bowman's arrival.

I only had a few moments before the elevator pinged and the doors opened, revealing Bowman and the two agents that had been with him. One of the agents was sporting what looked like a large burn on one arm; Alleam's energy shots must have struck closer than I had initially thought. He was limping, his gun arm hanging uselessly. The other agent seemed uninjured but rattled, his gun swinging wildly in all directions as he left the elevator. The Secret Service was excellently trained and capable of dealing with hundreds of different situations. Dealing with angels was not one of them.

Dealing with somebody that could throw large objects with his mind was another one.

In rapid succession, I sent chairs and tables flying in the direction of Bowman and the two agents. A table caught the uninjured agent across the forehead and dropped him like a sack of potatoes. The injured agent managed to avoid the first few pieces of furniture but found it impossible to get a moment to train his gun with his unwounded arm. Eventually he caught a chair in the solar plexus and went down against the wall, his gun clattering away to the side.

Bowman managed to avoid everything I had thrown effortlessly, sliding and dodging around all the incoming objects with such deftness of movement that I could barely follow him with my eye. As the onslaught abated, Bowman reached out both hands in the direction of the wall I hid behind and twisted his face in a snarl, sending a beam of pure blue energy in my direction. I wrenched my eyes open, my mind still not entirely back in my own body, and forced myself to move. I scrambled clumsily to my feet and threw myself further along the wall as the energy beam slammed into the bricks and destroyed the area that I had just been hidden in.

"Heathen!" I heard Bowman spit with hatred. I was on my back, my head swimming with confusion, my vision overlaid with the sights from my own eyes and the Second Sight's viewpoint from above my body. It was all I could to keep myself from vomiting from the nausea; I was barely in a position to deal with Bowman right now. I heard his footsteps approaching. "I gave you a chance to be part of the Lord's work!" he shouted again, the pitch of his voice rising hysterically. "And you choose to go against the word of your creator and help those who want to destroy the very fabric of our society!" He rounded the corner of the wall and stood over me, his face twisted in hatred and disappointment. "You could have been such a help to our work," he said, softer and with a hint of sadness this time.

Behind me I could hear the helicopter's engines beginning to spool up. Bowman shook his head slowly. "But you failed, Sam," he said, his voice rising in volume again. "You think you and your hellish compatriots downstairs can stand up to the forces of God Almighty?" He laughed; a short, sharp bark. "You will learn the value of humility tonight, son," he said, raising a hand towards me. "And then you will die – and this time, there will be no return ticket."

I closed my eyes tightly, waiting for the oncoming pain of the energy blast. I felt myself bathed in heavenly blue light…

…but no pain was forthcoming. I opened my eyes and realised that the glowing blue was not from Bowman but from a place above our heads. A bright blue ball of energy was slowly descending towards us, its glow illuminating the entire city block like a miniature sun, causing me to raise a hand to protect my eyes. Bowman looked up and grinned. "Well now," he drawled, looking back down at me. "It looks like my cavalry has arrived to take care of your friends." He raised both hands above his head, basking in the glow. "Praise the Lord!" he shouted aloud, a fervent zeal in his voice. "He shall be our salvation!"

I laughed. It sounded strange in comparison to the intense religious belief of Bowman, almost jarring. He looked down at me in confusion. I pushed myself up into a seated position. "You're right about the salvation bit," I said, my voice croaking with exhaustion. The extensive use of my powers was catching up to me and my muscles screamed at me to let them rest. I forced myself into a crouching position at the feet of Bowman, who was staring at me in bewilderment. "But it's not you who's being saved." I looked up at him straight in the eyes. "Now," I said calmly. "Go to Hell."

Bowman's eyes widened with realisation, but it was too late. Above our heads, the blue light reshaped itself into the outline of Anahita, the glowing, rotating wheels of the Ophanim's mark shining from her forehead. She looked down at Bowman, her eyes ablaze like a pair of spotlights. Raising her head, she let out a scream of exertion and fury, the noise ringing in my ears.

The Ophanim's wheels glowed even brighter.

A brilliant light concentrated into a fine beam shot down from Anahita's glowing form and struck Bowman from above. He screamed, his voice joining Anahita's in a competing wail of different pitches as his body was engulfed in energy. I pushed myself back on my hands and feet as quickly as I could, trying to get as far away as possible from the heat and light of the attack.

There was no escape now.

Bowman continued to scream, thrashing his arms around within the glowing beam of energy. He fell slowly to one knee, his form beginning to sag as the strength left him. He lifted his head slowly, as if this simple gesture was the most difficult trial of his life, and glared at me with eyes flashing with anger and pain. He reached out one hand toward me laboriously. I flinched, expecting some kind of final attack, but none came. The beam became even brighter, the force of the angelic energies tearing into Bowman's body. His flesh began to boil in the intense heat, slaking off his bones as it was cooked. His face began to melt, and Bowman's outraged expression dissolved into nothing more than an ugly, gaping skull. The glow around his body reached a point of brightness where I could no longer see him, and his screams died away into thin air.

The beam cut out, returning the rooftop to the darkness of night as if plunged into the blackness of the void. I blinked repeatedly, the beam's after-image seared onto my retinas and splitting my vision in two. The world seemed deathly quiet. I pulled myself to my feet and stepped forward, looking down at the spot where Bowman had fallen. Nothing remained apart from a light coating of grey dust, lightly disturbed as I watched by a twilight breeze. I stood there, looking down at it for a long moment. "Ashes to ashes," I muttered wearily.

I limped across to check the pulses on Bowman's two Secret Service agents; they were alive but unconscious. A quick glance towards the helicopter told me that the pilot had freaked out and bailed sometime during the angelic destruction of his former boss. Groaning in pain, I pulled myself across to the front of the Peninsula's rooftop and looked down over the front of the façade. I made it there just in time to see the infernal bikers stop their attacks and speed away down the road and into the night, leaving a trail of destruction and wounded police officers behind them. The wail of sirens was drawing ever closer and I realised that every law enforcement member in the city would likely be on its way here. I turned back to the rooftop and watched the form of my guardian angel slowly land.

Anahita looked utterly exhausted. She staggered a little as she landed, holding out both arms to balance herself. The mark of the Ophanim faded away in that moment, leaving nothing but a flickering blue halo of light around her body. She looked up at me and smiled faintly. "All in a day's work," she said with a forced, light-hearted tone. Then she keeled over onto her back.

I ran over to her and knelt by her side. The blue aura had completely left her now and she was breathing rhythmically, peacefully. I smiled affectionately and brushed a few strands of hair from her eyes. Over my shoulder, I felt Alleam's presence as he materialised. I looked up and saw him staring at her with concern in his eyes. "She will live," he said quietly, although his voice suggested a degree of worry that I did not like. "In the meantime, we need to be leaving."

I nodded. I could hear helicopters approaching and the sounds of police sirens were almost on top of us now. "I don't know how they're going to explain this," I said, nodding to the pile of ash that used to be the second-most senior politician in the United States.

"Not our problem," Alleam said shortly, placing one arm gently on my shoulder. "We have done our part to keep this world intact today."

"Amen to that," I muttered. I closed my eyes and felt Alleam teleport us away from the hotel.

Chapter 20

It was three days before I saw Alleam again.

I was standing on the balcony of Norman's quarters, overlooking the gardens behind the commune building. Neither my home nor my place of work were safe after everything that had happened, so in the aftermath of the events at the Peninsula it seemed safest for me to take refuge with Norman and his band of followers. Alleam had taken Anahita into his care and disappeared into the ether, promising to return. I had spent most of my time reading and helping in the gardens; the manual work felt good, and the simple day-to-day living of the people around me was something I was getting increasingly comfortable with. I had still not seen Miriam yet; she was in secluded care in an area of the commune that was explained to me as "a place for the most lost" by Norman. It troubled me greatly; the effects of her experience in Hell were evidently much more long-term than I had feared. I was musing upon this as I watched the sun go down when I felt Alleam's presence behind me. I turned and looked at him for a long moment in silence. Eventually I said, "So what's the situation?"

Alleam sighed. He looked tired and he rubbed his forehead in a very human manner. "Anahita is resting," he said. "It will take a while for her to be back to her previous strength levels, so you will have to do without a guardian angel for a while." He looked out across the gardens. "From what I understand," he continued, "the death of your country's Vice-President and the attack on the Peninsula are being treated as some kind of major terrorist event." He smiled and shook his head slightly. "It always impresses me how easily humanity can ignore the supernatural when it happens right in front of them."

I smiled. "It's a gift of our species," I observed, leaning on the guardrail that ringed the balcony. "When it comes to knowing about the terrifying beings of power that are fighting for our souls, I'd say that ignorance is sometimes most definitely bliss." I glanced at Alleam. "What about the fallout between the supernatural factions?" I asked.

"It's mostly been covered up," Alleam replied. "The Hellish forces are categorically denying that they had anything to do with the attack on the Horseman and Heaven cannot afford to push the issue too far right now, despite being pretty sure of what the truth is." He smiled. "Right now, the official line is that my rebel group is simply much larger than originally expected."

I snorted, shaking my head. "Politics," I observed. "Wherever you are, it's always the same."

We stood in silence for a while, basking in the dying embers of sunlight. Presently, Alleam spoke again. "It is a good idea for you to continue remaining out of sight of the terrestrial and Heavenly authorities," he said. "The Heavenly faction will be very much trying to track you down right now." "I'll need some things from my home," I replied.

Alleam nodded. "We can arrange that."

We lapsed into silence again. Then I said, "I need to be more in the loop."

Alleam turned to me and blinked slowly. "I'm sorry?" he asked.

I looked Alleam in the eye. "I'm much deeper into this by now then you intended," I said calmly. "You will need me again in tracking down the next three Horsemen as they appear." I shrugged slightly. "I also seem to have powers further-reaching than you anticipated. That makes me a valuable asset to your objectives, and that means I need to be more in the loop."

Alleam looked at me for a long moment. "There is grave

danger in following the path you have started on," he said slowly. "You have already been touched far more by the influence of Hell than I ever wished for. The further development of your powers will make things even harder for you to control, and you'll be subject to even more risks and dangers."

I smiled. "Three days ago I fought a Horseman of the Apocalypse," I replied. "How much more dangerous can it get than that?"

"Losing your soul," Alleam said quietly.

I opened my mouth and then closed it again. "You're right," I eventually admitted. "But everything we do has the potential to damage our soul." I looked at Alleam critically. "That's why your boss gave us free will, isn't it?" I pointed out. "So we could choose our own path in life and follow what we felt was best for us?" I looked back out across the gardens, watching the people several stories below picking crops for the next month's food supply. "You said so yourself," I observed. "We're in a literal fight for the world we exist in. You need all the help you can get."

Alleam was silent, which I took as a grudging acquiescence. "It will only get harder," he said quietly.

I smirked, my eyes fixed on the setting sun. "It only ever does," I replied.

Alleam had no reply, so we just stood there on the balcony; a renegade angel and a descendant of a forsaken Nephilim, staring in appreciation at the same world and sharing the same desire to keep it safe.

I just hoped we could.

THE END.

About the Author

C.J. Somersby is an author who resides in Nottingham in the UK. He graduated from Nottingham Trent University with a Masters in Science in Management & International Business in 2012.

He enjoys the finer things in life like world domination, good alcohol and getting his thoughts scribbled down in some form of order to hopefully turn into a book.

This book is his debut, and the result of too many late nights and not enough coffee.

A Selection of Other Publications from Dagda Publishing

Zero – J.S. Collyer

"Star Wars, Star Trek, Stargate, Firefly, Farscape and all. Zero certainly aims high"

To Touch The Sun – Laura Enright

"Adding a clever twist to all the popular vampire legends, Laura shows how even a well-worn genre can still carry a good story"

Fretensis – Dennis Villelmi

"At points I made notes to myself like "Ballard," "noir," "Nietzsche," "Carver," "Blake," "Burroughs," as I reached for some comparison. There are elements of the surreal and the absurd and a willingness to dive into madness that called to mind Artaud."

To The Lions – Claire Meadows

"Claire Meadows takes her reader on a dark and at times savage journey through a smouldering, hellish world where smoke, fire, illusion and disillusion play their part, obscuring the light, keeping the voice in a state of perpetual darkness."

The Pustoy – Philippe Blenkiron

"'The Pustoy' captures and reflects so many moods such that that (at times) it puts me in mind of T S Eliot and (at other times) one of the Hebrew prophets. There is no self-indulgence here."

For all our titles, please visit: www.dagdapublishing.co.uk/shop

11589025R00115

Printed in Great Britain
by Amazon.co.uk, Ltd.,
Marston Gate.